Tarlton's Jests: A Retelling

David Bruce

Published by David Bruce, 2022.

COVER PHOTO for *Tarlton's Jests*: A Retelling

https://pixabay.com/en/costume-middle-ages-musician-2512106/

Do you know a language other than English? If you do, I give you permission to translate this book, copyright your translation, publish or self-publish it, and keep all the royalties for yourself. (Do give me credit, of course, for the original retelling.)

This is a work of fiction. Similarities to real people, places, or events are entirely coincidental.

TARLTON'S JESTS: A RETELLING

First edition. July 20, 2022.

Copyright © 2022 David Bruce.

ISBN: 979-8201237899

Written by David Bruce.

Table of Contents

Dedication

Dedicated to My Uncle Reuben Saturday

When he was a young man, my mother's brother Reuben wanted to escape from poverty and lard sandwiches, so he tried to run away from it. He stole a car so he could drive up north where he hoped to find opportunity, but he got caught and ended up on a Georgia chain gang for several months. In a chain gang, prisoners are shackled every few feet by the ankles to a long length of chain to keep them from escaping. They work in the hot sun while shackled to the chain, and when they sleep, they are shackled to the bed. No freedom, hard work, hot sun, no pay, bad food, and some mean guards.

When my uncle got released from the chain gang, he hitchhiked up north. He did what a lot of people trying to escape from poverty do: He drifted. He drifted from town to town, seeking opportunity and not finding it. He worked when he could, but the jobs were temporary and low pay. My uncle slept rough often, and he was hungry often. Once, when he was completely broke and completely hungry, he saw a restaurant with a buffet and went inside and asked to speak to the manager. He said, "I am very hungry, I don't have any money, and I would appreciate it very much if you would give me any food that the restaurant is going to throw away. I will be happy to wait by the rear entrance until you are ready to throw away food."

The manager told him to sit down at a table, and then the manager went to the buffet, loaded a big plate high with food, and gave it to him free of charge.

One way out of poverty is to get a good job, and my uncle got out of poverty by getting a job working with sheet metal.

My uncle's work ethic helped him. His employer sent him to California to do some special sheet-metal work, and the people in California wanted to keep him there. They explained that their

California employees liked to come to work late, leave early, and take many days off. It was difficult to get someone who would show up and do the work they were supposed to do and were paid to do.

My uncle was also good with money. He got married, bought a house, and raised six children. Each time he made a mortgage payment, he paid extra money so he could pay off the mortgage faster.

If there was a sale on food, he bought lots of it. He had a large pantry, and if there was a sale on peanut butter, two jars for the price of one, he would buy twelve jars and sometimes go back the next day and buy six more jars.

If you went in his pantry — a closet set aside to store food — you saw that it was packed with food. If you went in his kitchen, you saw that he had taken off the doors of the high cabinets in which he stored food so that he could see the food. If you went in his bedroom, you saw that he had all the regular bedroom furniture, but he also had lots of shelves he had installed. The shelves were loaded with things that he had bought on sale that he knew his family could use: food (of course), light bulbs, toothpaste, toilet paper, etc. His bedroom looked like a warehouse.

Once he made a bad purchase: he bought a case of baked beans. Beans are beans, but the sauce they came in can taste good or bad, and the sauce these beans came in tasted bad. His kids told him, "Dad, throw those beans away! They're awful!"

But when you grow up poor, you don't throw beans away. For a long time, whenever my uncle and his family ate baked beans, they ate a mixture of one can of good baked beans and one can of bad baked beans.

My uncle's kids never had to eat lard sandwiches.
***
The doing of good deeds is important. As a free person, you can choose to live your life as a good person or as a bad person. To be a good person, do good deeds. To be a bad person, do bad deeds.

If you do good deeds, you will become good. If you do bad deeds, you will become bad. To become the person you want to be, act as if you already are that kind of person. Each of us chooses what kind of person we will become. To become a good person, do the things a good person does. To become a bad person, do the things a bad person does. The opportunity to take action to become the kind of person you want to be is yours.

Preface

TARLTON, RICHARD (d. 1588), English actor, was probably at one time an inn-keeper, but in 1583, when he is mentioned as one of the original company of The Queen's Players, was already an experienced actor. He was Elizabeth's favourite clown, and his talent for impromptu doggerel on subjects suggested by his audience has given his name to that form of verse. To obtain the advantage of his popularity a great number of songs and witticisms of the day were attributed to him, and after his death *Tarlton's Jests*, many of them older than he, made several volumes. Other books, and several ballads, coupled his name with their titles. He is said to have been the Yorick of Hamlet's soliloquy.

***

Public Domain Source:

Chisholm, Hugh, ed. (1911). "Tarlton, Richard". *Encyclopædia Britannica*. 26 (11th ed.). Cambridge University Press.

https://en.wikisource.org/wiki/1911_Encyclopædia_Britannica/Tarlton,_Richard

***

Notes:

Richard Tarlton died in 1588.

One of Tarlton's jests was a story about his clothes being stolen, something that happens to Bartholomew Cokes in Ben Jonson's *Bartholomew Fair*. Tarlton is mentioned in that play.

The author of *Tarlton's Jests* is anonymous.

Chapter I: Tarlton's Court-Witty Jests.

1. How Tarlton Played the Drunkard Before the Queen.

Tarlton once noticed that Queen Elizabeth I was unhappy, and he took it upon himself to delight her with some quaint jest. Therefore, he pretended to be drunk, and he called loudly for beer, which was brought immediately to him. Her Majesty, noticing what appeared to be his drunkenness, commanded that he should have no more beer because, she said, "He will act like a beast, and so shame himself."

Tarlton said to her, "You need not be afraid of that, for your beer is small enough."

Hearing this, her Majesty laughed heartily and commanded that he should have enough.

Note:

Small beer is weak beer.

2. How Tarlton Deceived the Watchmen in Fleet Street.

Having recently been at court and coming homewards through Fleet Street, Tarlton saw the watchmen, and not knowing how to pass them, he went very fast, thinking by that means to go past them without being questioned. But because the watchmen saw that he shunned them, they went to him and commanded him in the name of the Queen to stand.

Tarlton said, "Stand? Let them stand who can, for I cannot."

He then fell down, as though he were drunk, and the watchmen helped him up and let him pass.

3. How Tarlton Mocked a Lady in the Court.

Tarlton was among certain ladies at a banquet at Greenwich while Queen Elizabeth I was staying there. One of the ladies had her face full of pimples and she had heat at her stomach, for which reason she refused to drink wine among the rest of the ladies, which Tarlton perceiving (for he was there with the purpose to jest among them), he said, "A marren of that face, which makes all the body fare the worse for it."

Hearing this, the rest of the ladies laughed, and she (blushing for shame) left the banquet.

Note:

The word "marren" may refer to three things: 1) marring — the pimples mar her face, 2) marine — her face mars her stomach, as if she were seasick, and 3) murrain, aka plague.

4. Tarlton's Opinion of Oysters.

While certain noblemen and ladies of the court were eating oysters, one of them saw Tarlton, called to him, and asked him if he loved oysters.

"No," Tarlton replied, "for they are an ungodly, uncharitable, and unprofitable food."

"Why is that?" asked the courtiers.

"They are ungodly," Tarlton replied, "because they are eaten without grace; uncharitable, because they leave nothing but shells; and unprofitable, because they must swim in wine."

5. Tarlton's Resolution of a Question.

One of the company taking the gentleman's part, asked Tarlton at what time he thought the Devil to be the busiest.

"When the Pope dies," Tarlton replied.

"Why?" the courtier asked.

"Indeed," he said, "when the Pope dies all the Devils are troubled and busied to plague the Pope, for he has sent many a soul before him to Hell, who exclaim against him."

Note:

Many people in England during Tarlton's time were against the Pope.

6. How a Parsonage Fell into Tarlton's Hands.

When her Majesty Elizabeth I dined in the Strand at the Lord Treasurer's, the lords were very desirous that she would vouchsafe to stay all night, but nothing could prevail with her. Tarlton was in his clown's apparel and staying all dinner in her presence to make her merry, and hearing the sorrow that the noblemen expressed because they could not persuade her to stay, he asked the nobles what they would give him to persuade her to stay. The lords promised him anything to perform it.

Tarlton said, "Procure for me the Parsonage of Shard."

The lords caused the patent to be drawn immediately, and Tarlton put on a parson's gown and a corner-cap, and standing upon the stairs where the Queen would descend, he repeated these words: "A Parson, or no Parson? A Parson, or no Parson?"

The Queen, after she knew his meaning, not only stayed all night, but the next day willed that he should have possession of the benefice.

No parson was ever madder than Tarlton, for he threatened to turn the bell-metal into money to fill his purse, which he did; in fact, he turned the parsonage and all in it into ready money with which to fill his purse.

Note:

The word "vouchsafe" means to confer a benefit on a person.

7. How Tarlton Proved [One of] Two Gentlewomen Dishonest by Their Own Words.

Seeing in Greenwich two gentlewomen in the garden together, Tarlton to cause mirth went to them and enquired, "Gentlewomen, which of you two is the honester?"

"I am," one said. "I hope that I am honest without exceptions."

The other gentlewoman said, "I am the honester, since we must speak for ourselves."

Tarlton then said, "One of you by your own words is dishonest, because one of you must be honester than the other, else you would answer otherwise, but as I found you, so I leave you."

Note:

"Honest" can mean "chaste" as well as the usual meaning.

8. How Tarlton Answered a Wanton Gentlewoman.

A merrily disposed gentlewoman, being crossed by Tarlton, and half angry, said, "Sirrah, a little thing would make me requite you with a cuff."

"With a cuff, Lady?" Tarlton says. "So you would spell my sorrow forward, but if you instead spell my sorrow backward, then cuff me and don't spare me."

When the gentlemen nearby thought about the word "cuff," they laughed and made the simple-meaning gentlewoman blush for shame.

Notes:

The gentlewoman threatened to cuff, aka hit, Tarlton.

The joke seems to be in the word "cuff." Spelled backward, the word is "ffuc," and so Tarlton is saying, "So you would spell my sorrow forward, but spell my sorrow backward, then f**k me and don't spare me."

The gentlewoman is "simple-meaning" because her use of the word "cuff" had one meaning. Tarlton is capable of wordplay.

"Sirrah" is a way of addressing a man of lower social rank than the speaker.

9. How Tarlton Dared a Lady.

At a dinner in the great chamber where Tarlton jested, the ladies were daring one another. One lady said, "I always dare do anything that is honest and honorable."

Tarlton said, "I bet a French crown that's not true."

The lady replied, "I bet ten pounds it is true."

Tarlton said, "Done."

The lady replied, "Done."

Tarlton put two pence between his lips, daring her to take it away with her lips.

"Bah," the lady said. "That is immodesty."

"What? To kiss is immodest?" Tarlton said. "Then immodesty bears a great hand over all [for all have kissed]. Just this once in your life, say that you have been beaten at your own weapon."

"Well, sir," she said. "You may say anything."

Tarlton said, "Remember, I said you dare not, and so my wager is good."

10. How Tarlton Landed at Cuckolds Haven.

Tarlton, because he stayed one Sunday at court all day, caused a pair of oars [rowers, aka watermen] to tend him, who at night called on him to be gone. Tarlton, being in a carousing mood, drank so long to and with the watermen that one of them was bumpsy [intoxicated], and so indeed were all three for the most part. At last they left Greenwich, the tide being at a great low point. The watermen, who were still afraid of the cross-cables on the Thames River by the Lime House, very dark and late as it was, landed Tarlton at Cuckolds Haven, and said that the next day they would give him a reason for it. But Tarlton was eager to go by land to Redriffe on the dirty bank, although every step was knee-deep in mud, so that on coming home, he called one of his boys to help him off with his boots, meaning his stockings, which were dyed of another color. Whereupon one gave him this theme the next day:

> Tarlton, tell me, for fain would I know [eager am I to know],
> If [Whether] you were landed at Cuckolds Haven or no?

Tarlton answered thus:

> Yes, sir, and I take it in no scorn:
> For many land there yet miss having the horn.

Notes:

Possibly, Tarlton's stockings were "dyed" with the color of mud. Possibly, Tarlton had lost his boots in the mud.

Cuckolds were said to have invisible horns growing from their foreheads.

Cables are the thick ropes used to raise and lower anchors.

Tarlton's doggerel says that a man can land at Cuckolds Haven although he is not a cuckold.

A theme is a topic. In this anecdote, it is a topic for a jest.

11. How Tarlton Fought with Black Davie.

Once there lived a little swaggerer called Black Davie, who would with sword and buckler fight any gentleman or other man for twelve pence. He once was hired to draw his sword against Tarlton because Tarlton had made a jest at the expense of Huffing Kate, as men called her. She was a punk, aka prostitute.

One evening, Tarlton came forth from the court gate, being at Whitehall, and walking toward the tilt-yard, a place where tournaments were held, this Davie immediately drew his sword against Tarlton, who immediately, although amazed and surprised, drew his sword likewise, and asked the reason for Black Davie's drawing his sword against him. Black Davie declined to answer the question until they had fought a bout or two.

Tarlton courageously got within Black Davie's defenses, and taking him in his arms, threw him into the tilt-yard. Black Davie, falling upon his nose, broke it extremely, so that ever afterward he snuffled in the head; poor Davie lay all that night in the tilt-yard, waiting for the doors to be opened. He came forth, and at the barber-surgeon's told of this bloody combat.

The reason for the combat was, he said, because Tarlton had been in a tavern, and in the company of this damnable cockatrice, Huffing Kate, called for wine, but she told him that unless he would burn it, she would not drink.

"No," Tarlton said, "I won't burn it, but it shall be burnt, for you can burn it without fire."

"How, sir?" Huffing Kate asked.

"Indeed, like this," Tarlton said. "Take the cup in your hand, and I will tell you."

Black Davie then said, "So he filled the cup in her hand, and said it was burnt sufficiently in so fiery a place. She, perceiving herself so flouted, hired me to be her champion, to revenge her quarrel."

Notes:

"Huffing" means blustering.

A cockatrice is a woman of bad character.

A hot whore is a whore who is burning from venereal disease. The joke is that Huffing Kate is so hot from venereal disease that the wine in the cup in her hand burns.

Burning is a name for the distillation of wine.

To flout a person is to mock that person.

12. How Tarlton, Coming from the Court, Answered the Watchmen.

Tarlton, having played before the Queen until one o'clock after midnight, was walking homewards.

One of the watchmen spied him, and called to him, "Sirrah, who are you?"

"A woman," Tarlton, who had a beard or at least stubble at the time, replied.

"No, that is a lie," said the watchmen. "Women have no such beards."

Tarlton replied, "If I should have said that I am a man, that is something that you know to be true, and you would have told me to tell you something that you do not know, and so therefore I said that I am a woman, and so in fact I am all woman because I have pleased the Queen, being a woman."

"Well, sirrah," says another watchman, "I present [represent] the Queen."

One meaning of presenting the Queen is imitating the Queen or acting the role of the Queen, as if on stage.

"Then I am a woman, indeed," says Tarlton, "as well as you, for you have a beard as well as I, and truly, Mistress Annis, my busk is not done yet: When will yours be done?"

A busk is either a corset or a piece of wood or whalebone used to stiffen a corset.

"Stop your joking, fellow," said the watchman. "The Queen's will is that whosoever is taken out of doors after ten o'clock, shall be committed to jail, and now it is past one."

"Commit all such," says Tarlton, "for if it be past one o'clock, it will not be ten for these eight hours."

With that one of the watchmen lifted up his lantern, and looked Tarlton in the face, and recognized him and said, "Indeed, Mr. Tarlton, you have more wit than all of us watchmen, for it is true that ten was before one, but now one is before ten."

"That is true," said Tarlton. "Watchmen had used to have more wit, but for want of sleep they are turned fools."

So Tarlton stole away from them, and in order to seem wise the watchmen went home to bed.

Note:

Tarlton said that he is all woman because he pleased the Queen, "being a woman." Did he mean that only a woman could please Queen Elizabeth I? Possibly, he had played the role of a woman on stage for the Queen.

13. Tarlton's Answer to a Courtier.

Tarlton, after being at the court all night, in the morning met a great courtier coming from his bedchamber, who seeing Tarlton, said, "Good morning, Mr. Didimus and Tridimus."

Tarlton being somewhat abashed, not knowing the meaning of this greeting, said, "Sir, I don't understand you. Explain the meaning of what you said, please."

The courtier replied, "Didimus and Tridimus is a fool and a knave."

"You overload me," replied Tarlton, who was a professional Fool, "for my back cannot bear both; therefore, you take the one, and I will take the other. You take the knave, and I will carry the Fool with me."

Notes:

"*Didymus*" is French for "testicule," aka testicle.

According to the OED [*Oxford English Dictionary*], "didymis" is an obsolete term for testicles.

"Trismus" occurs when the jaw muscles clench and keep the jaws tightly closed, as when the person has tetanus.

Perhaps the names Didimus and Tridimus came from legal terminology:

According to the OED, "dedimus" is "A writ empowering one who is not a judge to do some act in place of a judge."

According to the OED, "vidimus" is "A copy of a document bearing an attestation that it is authentic or accurate."

14. Tarlton's Quip for a Young Courtier.

A young gentleman in the court, who had first lain [had first had sex] with the mother, and afterward with the daughter, asked Tarlton what it resembled.

Tarlton replied, "As if you would first have eaten the hen, and afterward, the chick."

15. Tarlton's Answer to a Nobleman's Question.

A nobleman asked Tarlton what he thought of soldiers in time of peace.

"Indeed," Tarlton said, "they are like chimneys in the summer."

16. Tarlton's Jest to an Unthrifty Courtier.

An unthrifty gallant belonging to the court, who had borrowed five pounds from Tarlton but lost it gambling with dice, sent his manservant to Tarlton to borrow five pounds more by using the same token by which he owed him already five pounds.

"Please tell your Master," Tarlton said, "that if he will send me a new token, I will send him the money because whoever deceives me once, may God forgive him; if he deceives me twice, may God forgive him; but if he deceives me thrice, may God forgive him but not forgive me, because I could not beware."

17. How Tarlton Flouted Two Gallants.

Tarlton, who was in a merry mood, walked in the Great Hall in Greenwich, where he met my old Lord Chamberlain walking between two fantastic gallants who were supporting him. Tarlton cried aloud to him, "My Lord, my Lord, you go in great danger."

Amazed, my old Lord Chamberlain asked, "In great danger of what?"

Tarlton said, "In great danger of drowning, were it not for those two bladders under each of your arms."

Chapter II: Tarlton's Sound City Jests.

18. Tarlton's Jest about a Red Face.

Gentlemen often dined at a certain tavern in White Friars because of the extraordinary diet of food served there. Tarlton often frequented this tavern as much to continue acquaintance with the gentlemen as to please his appetite. It chanced once that as he sat among the gentlemen and gallants, they asked him, "Why has melancholy gotten the upper hand of your mirth?"

To this he said little, but with a squint eye (as his customary way of life had made him hare-eyed) he looked for a jest to make them merry. At last he saw a man who sat on his left side and who had a very red face; that man was a very great gentleman (which was all one to Tarlton).

Tarlton immediately in great haste called his host and asked him, "Whom do I serve?"

The host replied, "The Queen's Majesty."

Tarlton then said, "How does it happen then, that to her Majesty's disgrace you dare make me a companion with serving men, clapping my Lord Shandoyes' cullisance, aka badge of arms, upon my sleeve," while looking at the gentleman with the red face. "I think," Tarlton said, "that it fits like the Saracen's Head outside Newgate."

The gentleman's salamander-red face burned like Mount Etna because of anger. The rest laughed heartily. In the end, the enraged gentleman swore to fight Tarlton the next time he met him.

Notes:

"Hare-eyed" means round eyes, or eyes that are never closed. Tarlton's eyes were always open in search of a jest.

"All one to Tarlton" means "Tarlton didn't care."

Lord Shandoyes' cullisance, aka badge of arms, is apparently red. Servants wore their master's arms upon their left arm as a form of identification. The insult seems to be in part a comparison between the gentleman's red face and Lord Shandoyes' cullisance.

The Saracen's Head outside Newgate was an inn.

The insult also seems to be in part a comparison between the gentleman's red face and the depiction of Saracens' heads on the sign of the Saracen's Head, an inn. These heads were called "huge, big, terrible faces" in *Selden's Table Talk*. *Osborn's Works* include this passage: "At the Saracen's Head, Tom pour'd in ale and wine, Until his face did represent the sign." The gentleman with the red face has done the same thing.

Tarlton is saying that he serves the Queen, not Lord Shandoyes.

Some quotations:

Do not undervalue an enemy by whom you have been worsted. When our countrymen came home from fighting with the Saracens, and were beaten by them, they pictured them with huge, big, terrible faces (as you still see the sign of the Saracen's Head is), when in truth they were like other men. But this they did to save their own credits. — Selden's Table Talk.

At the Saracen's Head, Tom pour'd in ale and wine, Until his face did represent the sign. — Osborn's Works, 8vo, 1701, p. 538.

Near to the jail, and by consequence near to Smithfield ... and on that particular part of Snow Hill, where omnibus horses going eastward seriously think of falling down on purpose, and where horses in hackney cabriolets going westward not unfrequently fall by accident, is the coachyard of the Saracen's Head Inn; its portal guarded by two Saracens' heads and shoulders ... frowning upon you from each side of the gateway. The Inn itself garnished with another Saracen's head, frowns upon you from the top of the yard. — Charles Dickens, *Nicolas Nickleby*.

19. A Sudden and Dangerous Fray Between a Gentleman and Tarlton, Which He Put Off with a Jest.

As Tarlton and others passed along Fleet Street, he saw a spruce young gallant, black of complexion, with long hair hanging down over his ears, and his beard of the Italian cut, wearing white satin, very quaintly cut, and his clothing so stiffly starched that he could not bend himself any way for any amount of gold. Tarlton, seeing such a wonder coming, walked quickly before him, and meeting this gallant, took the wall of him (he walked next to the wall, which is the prerogative of the person of higher social status), knowing that one so proud at least looked for the prerogative of taking the wall. The gallant scorning that a player (an entertainer) should take the wall and so much indignify — that is, insult — him, turned his whole body, and immediately drew his rapier. Tarlton drew his rapier likewise. The gentleman fell to it roundly, but Tarlton (in his own defense) compassing and traversing his ground, gaped [opened his mouth] with a wide mouth, whereat the people laughed. The gentleman paused and enquired why he gaped so.

"Oh, sir," Tarlton said, "in hope to swallow you, for truly you seem to me like a prune in a mess of white broth."

At this the people parted them. The gentleman, noting Tarlton's mad humor, went on his way well contented, for he did not know how to reply to it.

Notes:

Tarlton knew how to fence well.

A mess is a serving of food.

20. Tarlton's Jest about a Pippin.

At the Bull, an inn in Bishopsgate Street, where the Queen's Players often played, Tarlton coming on the stage, someone from the gallery threw a pippin at him. Tarlton took up the pip, and looking on it, made this sudden jest:

Pip in, or nose in, choose you whether [which],
Put yours in, ere [before] I put in the other.
Pippin you have put in: then, for my grace,
Would I [I wish I] might put your nose in another place.

Notes:

A pip or pippen is a small, hard seed. It can also be a kind of apple or a grape.

"Another place" is the stinkiest part of Tarlton's body.

21. A Jest about an Apple Hitting Tarlton on the Face.

Tarlton having flouted and insulted the fellow for his pippin that he threw, the fellow thought to get even with Tarlton at length. In the play Tarlton's part was to experience some travail, and at one point when he was kneeling down to ask his father for his blessing, the fellow threw an apple at him, which hit him on the cheek. Tarlton taking up the apple, made this jest:

> Gentleman, this fellow, with this face of mapple,
> Instead of a pippin, has thrown me an apple,
> But as for an apple, he has thrown a crab,
> So instead of an honest woman, God has sent him a drab.

The people laughed heartily, for the fellow had a quean to his wife.

Notes:

"Mapple" may come from the Latin *mappula*. If so, it means a table-napkin or handkerchief.

"Mapple" is also an obsolete name for a mop.

A crab apple is a sour species of apple.

A drab is a slut and/or an untidy woman.

An honest woman is a faithful woman.

A quean is a hussy, an impudent woman. Sometimes, a quean is a prostitute.

22. How Tarlton and Someone in the Gallery Fell Out.

It chanced that in the midst of a play, after long waiting to see Tarlton, whom the people much desired to see, at length he came forth. At his entrance, someone in the gallery pointed his finger at him and said to a friend who had never seen him, "That is Tarlton."

Tarlton enjoyed making a joke at the least occasion given him. Seeing the man point with his finger, Tarlton with malice aforethought held up two fingers. The captious fellow, jealous of his wife (for he was married) and because an entertainer did it, took the matter all the more heinously, and asked him why he made horns at him.

Tarlton said, "No. They aren't horns. They are fingers."

He then said:

> For there is no man, who in love to me,
> Lends me one finger, but he shall have three.

"No, no," says the fellow, "you gave me the horns."

"True," Tarlton said, "for my fingers are tipped with nails, which are like horns, and I must make a show of that which you are sure of."

This matter grew so, that the more the fellow meddled, the more it was for his disgrace, wherefore the bystanders counseled him to depart, both he and his horns, lest his cause grew desperate. So the poor fellow, plucking his hat over his eyes, went on his way.

Note:

The horns are the invisible horns said to grow on the forehead of a cuckold: a man with an unfaithful wife.

23. How Fiddlers Fiddled Away Tarlton's Apparel.

It chanced that one Fancy and Nancy, two musicians in London, used often with their singing boys to visit Tarlton when he dwelt in Gracious Street, at the sign of the Saba, a tavern, he being one of their best friends or benefactors, by reason of old acquaintance, to requite which they came one summer's morning to play for him "The Hunt's Up" [the name of the tune played to wake the hunters and collect them together. The name was also used for any morning song] with such music [musical instruments] as they had.

Tarlton, to requite them, would open his chamber door, and for their pains would give them Muscatine [Muscadine] wine, which a cony-catcher [a sharper, a cheat] noting, and seeing Tarlton come forth in his shirt and nightgown to drink with these musicians, this nimble fellow stepped in and took Tarlton's apparel, which Tarlton wore everyday, [the thief] thinking that if he were espied to pretend it was a jest, but it passed for current [he got away with it] and he went on his way.

Not long afterward, Tarlton returned to his chamber, and looked for his clothes, but they were safe enough from him. The next day this was noised [gossiped] abroad, and one in mockage threw him in this theme, he playing then at the Curtain:

Tarlton, I will tell thee a jest
Which after turned to earnest.
One there was, as I heard say.
Who in his shirt heard music play.
While all his clothes were stolen away.

Tarlton, smiling at this, answered on the sudden [ad-libbed] thus:

That's certain, sir, it is no lie.

That same one in truth was I.

When that the thief shall pine and lack,

Then shall I have clothes for my back:

And I, together with my fellows,

May see them ride to Tiborne gallows.

[May see the clothes, worn by Tarlton, ride to Tiborne gallows, where Tarlton and his friends will see the thief hang.]

24. Of Tarlton and a Beggar.

A poor beggar who was also a conceited [witty] fellow saw Tarlton at his door and asked for something from him for God's cause. Tarlton putting his hand in his pocket, gave him two pence instead of a penny, at which Tarlton made this rhyme:

Of all the beggars most happy you art [are],
For to thee my hand is better than my heart.

The Beggar replied:

True it is, Master, as it chances now:
The better for me, and the worse for you.

Note:
At the time, "conceited" meant witty and intelligent.

25. How Tarlton Deceived a Doctor of Physic [Medicine].

Tarlton, to satisfy the humors [moods] of certain gentlemen who were his familiar acquaintances, decided to test the skill of a simple Doctor of Physic, who dwelt not far from Islington, and this is what happened:

Tarlton took a urinal, filled it half full of good wine, and carried it to this doctor, saying it was a sick man's urine. The doctor viewed it, and tossing it up and down, as though he had great knowledge, he said that the patient whose urine it is, is full of gross humors, and has need of purging, and needs to be bled some ten ounces of blood.

"No, you dunce," Tarlton replied. "It is good piss," and he drank it all and then threw the urinal at the doctor's head.

Note:
Bloodletting was regarded as a way to restore health.

26. How Tarlton Frightened a Country Fellow.

While passing through London, Tarlton by chance heard a simple country fellow in an alehouse, calling for a Kingstone pot of ale. Tarlton stepped over to him and threatened to accuse him of treason, saying "Sirrah, I have seen and tasted of a penny pot of ale, and have found it good for the price of a penny coin, but I have never heard of a

Kingstone coin: therefore it is some counterfeit, and I must know how you came by it."

Hereupon, the country fellow was driven into such a maze, that out of doors he got, and took to his heels, as though wildfire had followed him.

27. How Tarlton was Deceived by His Wife in London.

Tarlton, being merrily disposed as his wife and he sat together, said to her, "Kate, answer for me one question, without a lie, and take this gold coin, which is a crown."

She took the gold coin on condition that if she lost, then she would give it back again.

Tarlton asked, "Am I a cuckold or not, Kate?"

Hearing this, she answered not a word, but stood silent, notwithstanding he urged her many times to answer his question. Tarlton, seeing she would not speak, asked for his gold coin again.

"Why," she said, "have I told any lie?"

"No," Tarlton said.

"Why then, good man fool, I have won the wager."

Tarlton, mad with anger, made this rhyme:

As women in speech can revile a man,
So can they in silence beguile a man.

Note:

Kate's answer was silence; keeping silent is a good way not to tell a lie.

28. Someone Asked Tarlton What Countryman the Devil Was.

In Carter Lane dwelt a merry cobbler, who being in company with Tarlton, asked him what countryman the Devil was.

Tarlton answered, "A Spaniard, because Spaniards, like the Devil, trouble the whole world."

Note:

The English navy defeated the Spanish Armada in 1588, the year Tarlton died.

29. A Cheesemonger's Question to Tarlton.

During a time of scarcity, a simple cheesemonger who had heard Tarlton commended for his quick wit came to him and asked him why he thought cheese and butter were so dear [expensive].

Tarlton answered, "Because wood and coals are so dear, for cheese and butter a man may eat without a fire."

Notes:

A cheesemonger sells cheese and butter.

The joke seems to be a pun on "dear," which can mean 1) expensive, or 2) loved. The cheesemonger asks why cheese and butter are so expensive. Tarlton answers that cheese and butter are loved because they can be eaten without also paying for a fire to cook them, which would have made the meal even more expensive.

30. Tarlton's Answer to a Rich Londoner.

Tarlton met a rich Londoner and fell into talk about the Bishop of Peterborough. Tarlton highly praised the good Bishop's bounty to his servants, his liberality to strangers, his great hospitality, and his charity to the poor.

"He does good deeds," the rich man said, "because what he has, he has only during his life."

Tarlton asked, "For how many lives will you have your goods?"

31. How Tarlton Gave Away His Dinner.

As Tarlton and his wife sat at dinner, his wife being displeased with him, and thinking to cross him, she gave away half his food to a poor beggar, saying, "Take this for my other husband's sake."

Immediately, Tarlton took all the food that was left and gave it to the poor beggar and likewise bade the poor fellow to pray for his other wife's soul.

32. Tarlton's Answer to a Boy in a Rhyme.

A crackrope boy, upon meeting Tarlton in London Street, sang this rhyme to Tarlton:

Woe worth thee, Tarlton,
That ever thou was born:
Thy wife has made thee a cuckold,
And thou must wear the horn.

Tarlton immediately answered him *ex tempore*:

What if I am, boy,
I'm never the worse:
She keeps me like a gentleman,
With money in my purse.

Notes:

A crackrope boy is a rogue.

A crackrope boy is a boy about whom people joke that he seems destined for the gallows.

"Woe worth thee" means "woe has come to you."

33. How Tarlton Bade [Invited] Himself to Dinner to My Lord Mayor's.

A jest came in Tarlton's head about where to dine, and he thought, *In all that a man does, let him aim at the fairest, for surely if I invite myself to dine anywhere this day, it shall be to my Lord Mayor's.*

Upon thinking this, he went to the counter [prison], and entered his legal action against my Lord Mayor, who was presently told of it, and sent for him. Tarlton waited until dinnertime, and then he came and was admitted immediately.

"Mr. Tarlton," my Lord Mayor asked, "have you entered an action against me in the Poultry Counter?"

"My Lord," Tarlton asked, "have you entered an action against me in the Wood Street Counter?"

"Truly, I have not," my Lord Mayor said.

"No!" Tarlton said. "He was a villain who told me that you had then, but if it be not so, forgive me this fault, my Lord, and I will never offend a next time."

But Tarlton then began to swear about how he would be revenged on the man who had mocked him by telling him a lie about my Lord Mayor, and he was ready to go out in a rage.

But my Lord Mayor said, "Stay, Master Tarlton, dine with me, and I have no doubt but after dinner you will be in a better mood."

"I will try that, my Lord Mayor," Tarlton said, "and if it lessens my anger, both my enemy and I will thank you together for this courtesy."

Notes:

The Poultry Country was a prison in London.

The Wood Street Counter was a small prison in London. It was used for such people as debtors. The prison was also referred to as the Wood Street Compter.

Both "counter" and "compter" mean prison.

34. Tarlton's Jest about a Box on the Ear.

A man who fell out with his friend met that friend in the street, and after calling him into a corner, he gave him a box on the ear, and felled him, and then fled, and never told the friend why he had hit him.

After seeing this, Tarlton raised up the fellow, and asked him the reason for their sudden falling out.

"Can you tell me, sir?" asked the fellow, "for truly as of now I cannot."

"Well," Tarlton said, "the more fool you, for if I had such feeling of the cause, my wit, aka intelligence, would remember the injury, but many men are goslings: The more they feel, the less they understand."

35. Tarlton's Jest to Two Tailors.

Meeting in the evening two tailors who were friends of his, Tarlton cried out in mirth, "Who goes there?"

"A man," answered a tailor.

"How many is there? One? Yes," Tarlton said.

"Two," said the other tailor.

"Then you say the truth," Tarlton said, "for two tailors go to a man."

But before they parted, the two tailors outfoxed Tarlton by making him drunk at the Castle in Pater Noster Row, with the result that Tarlton confessed that the two tailors were honest men.

So what the two tailors spent out of the purse, they got in the person. They spent money, but for the money, they got a compliment from their friend Tarlton.

Coming, they were only one, by Tarlton's account, but they returned as two. He had said that only one tailor was present when he first met them, but after drinking with him he said that two tailors were present.

But Tarlton, who had come to the Castle as one man, returned less than the man he was before he got drunk because his wit and intelligence shrank because of the wetting of his throat.

Note:

Tarlton said that two tailors make a man. The more usual expression now is "Nine tailors make a man." Thomas Dekker and John Webster wrote in their 1605 play *Northward Hoe*, "They say three tailors go to the making up of a man." The profession of tailor is one that Elizabethan and Jacobean playwrights mocked.

36. How Tarlton Jested at His Wife.

While Tarlton and his wife were staying at an ordinary [an inn] in Paternoster Row, they were invited out to supper, and because he was a famous man, his wife would not go with him in the street, but entreated him to keep to one side, and she would be on the other, which he consented to. But as he went, he would cry out to her, and say, "Turn that way, wife" and in a little while, "Go on this side, wife."

So the people flocked to them all the more to laugh at them. But his wife (more than insanely angry) went back home again, and almost forswore his company.

37. How Tarlton Committed a Raker's Horse to Ward [Prison].

When Tarlton dwelt in Gracious Street at a tavern at the sign of the Saba, he was chosen to be scavenger, and often the citizens of his ward complained of his slackness in keeping the streets clean. So at a time when the cart of the raker came, he asked the raker why he did his business so slackly.

"Sir," the raker said, "my fore-horse is at fault because it was let blood and drenched [dosed] with medicine yesterday, and I dared not work him."

"Sir," Tarlton said, "your horse shall smart for it."

Tarlton then led the horse to the counter [prison], which the raker laughed at, and without his horse did his work with the other rakers, thinking Tarlton's mood was only to jest, and Tarlton would return his horse to him again soon. But when "soon" came, he was obliged to pay all his fees of the prison as simply and plainly as if he himself had been there. For if Tarlton had committed the master, the business of cleaning the streets would not have gone forward; therefore, he had put the horse in prison in place of the master.

Notes:

A raker is someone who rakes the street to clean it.

A scavenger is someone whose job is to clean streets. Tarlton's job as scavenger seems to have been a supervisory position.

A counter is a prison.

38. How Tarlton Made Armin His Adopted Son to Succeed Him.

While Tarlton was keeping a tavern in Gracious Street, he rented it to another person, one who was indebted to Robert Armin's master, a goldsmith in Lombard Street, yet he himself had a chamber [room] in the same tavern. And this Armin, being then a wag, came often thither to demand his master's money, which the man renting the tavern sometimes had, and sometimes had not. In the end the man growing poor, he told the boy he had no money for his master, and he must bear with him. The man's name being Charles, Armin made this verse, writing it with chalk on a wainscot [wooden paneling].

> O world, why wilt thou lie?
> Is this Charles the great? That I deny.
> Indeed [he was] Charles the great before:
> But now [he is] Charles the less, being poor.

Tarlton, coming into the room, read it, and partly acquainted with the boy's humor because the boy had come often thither for his master's money, took a piece of chalk, and wrote this rhyme by it:

> A wag thou are, none can prevent thee;
> And thy desert shall content thee,
> Let me divine [tell the future]: As I am, so in time thou'lt be the same,
> My adopted son therefore be,
> To enjoy my clown's suit after me.

And see how it fell out. The boy, after reading Tarlton's words so loved Tarlton afterward that, regarding him with more respect, he used to [he observed] his plays, and fell in a league with his humor, and private practice brought him to present playing, and at this hour he performs comic roles and at the Globe Theater on the Bankside men may see him.

Notes:

Apparently, Tarlton rented the tavern to another man, but Tarlton kept a room at the tavern to stay in.

Robert Armin acted in William Shakespeare's plays. He frequently played the role of Fool.

Robert Armin probably originated these roles:

- Lavatch in *All's Well That Ends Well*
- Touchstone in *As You Like It*

- The Fool in *King Lear*
- The Porter in *Macbeth*
- The Fool in *Timon of Athens*
- Thersites in *Troilus and Cressida*
- Feste in *Twelfth Night*
- Autolycus in *The Winter's Tale*

He also appeared in Ben Jonson's *The Alchemist*.

39. Tarlton's Greeting with Banks' Horse.

In the time of Tarlton, a man named Banks served the Earl of Essex and had a horse of unusual tricks. Banks was staying at the Cross Keys Inn in Gracious Street, and he was getting money from displaying his horse's tricks, as many people wished to see the horse. Tarlton, who was then with his fellows playing at the Bell nearby, came into the Cross Keys Inn among many other people to see this horse that was fashionable to discuss.

Seeing all the people assembled, Banks — to make the people laugh — said to his horse, "Signior, go fetch me the greatest fool in the company."

The jade went immediately and with his mouth drew Tarlton out of the company of people. Tarlton said nothing but the merry words "God-a-mercy, horse."

But in the end Tarlton, seeing and hearing the people laugh at him, was angry inwardly, and he said to Banks, "Sir, if I had power over your horse, as you have, I would do more than that."

"Whatever it is you want," Banks said to please him, "I will order my horse to do it."

"Then," Tarlton said, "order him to bring me the greatest whoremaster in this company of people."

"He shall," Banks replied.

He then said to his horse, "Signior, bring Master Tarlton here the greatest whoremaster in the company."

His horse then used its mouth to bring Banks himself to Tarlton.

"Then God-a-mercy, horse, indeed," Tarlton said.

The people laughed and had much ado to keep peace, but Banks and Tarlton were close to fighting and the horse was nearby to remind them what they would be fighting about.

But ever afterward, "God-a-mercy, horse" was a byword through London, and it is to this day.

Notes:

According to the OED, "God-a-mercy horse" is "often used merely as a formulaic tag to a humorous story or anecdote."

Also according to the OED, "God-a-mercy" can be used to express thanks or applause, but it can also be used to express surprise or distress.

40. An Excellent Jest by Tarlton Suddenly Spoken.

At the Bull at Bishopsgate in London was a play titled *The Famous Victories of Henry the Fifth*, wherein the judge was to take a box on the ear, and because the actor was absent who should take the blow, Tarlton himself, who was always eager to please the audience, took it upon himself to play that same judge, besides his own part of the clown.

During a performance, the actor and comedian William Knell then playing King Henry the Fifth hit Tarlton a sound box indeed, which made the people laugh all the more because it was Tarlton, but soon the judge went offstage, and immediately Tarlton — in his clown's clothes — came out, and asked the actors, "What is the news?"

"Oh," an actor replied, "if you had been here, you would have seen Prince Henry hit the judge a terrible box on the ear."

"What man," Tarlton asked, "would strike a judge?"

"It is true indeed," the actor said.

"No other like," Tarlton said, "and it could not be but terrible to the judge, when the report so terrifies me that I think the blow remains still on my cheek, so that it burns again."

The people laughed at this mightily, and to this day I have heard it commended for rare wit, but it is no marvel that Tarlton had adlibbed this, for he made many adlibs like this. But I would like to see our clowns in these days be as good as Tarlton at adlibbing. They cannot, I promise you, and yet they think well of themselves, too.

41. Tarlton's Jest with a Boy in the Street.

A wag-halter boy met Tarlton in the street and asked him, "Master Tarlton, who lives longest?"

"Indeed, boy," Tarlton said, "he who dies latest."

"Why do men die so fast?" the boy asked.

"Because they lack breath," Tarlton said.

"No," the boy said. "Rather because their time has come."

"Then your time has come," Tarlton said. "Do you see who comes yonder?"

"Who?" the boy asked.

Tarlton replied, "Bull the Hangman, who is someone who would willingly be your hangman."

"Hang me then, if I employ him at this time," the boy said.

"Well said," Tarlton said. "Then you will be hanged by your own confession."

And so they parted.

Notes:

A wag-halter boy is a mischievous boy whom people say as a joke is likely to be hanged. Or possibly he is a mischievous stable boy.

The boy will not be hanged now, but apparently Tarlton jokes that he will be at a time of his choosing — that is, after he has confessed to a crime.

42. A Jest by Tarlton, Proving Mustard to have Wit.

Tarlton, who was staying in an inn in Paternoster Row and sitting with gentlemen to make them merry, said that he would prove that mustard (some of which was on the table before them) has wit and intelligence.

"How can you do that?" a gentleman asked.

"It is like a witty scold, meeting another scold, knowing that the other scold will scold, and so begins to scold first," Tarlton said. "The mustard being licked up, and knowing that you will bite it, begins to bite you first."

"I'll try that," a nearby fool said.

He swallowed some mustard, and the mustard so tickled his throat that his eyes watered.

"What do you think now?" Tarlton asked. "Does my jest have savor?"

"Aye," the fool said, "and it has bite, too."

"If you had had better wit and intelligence," Tarlton said, "you would have bit first, so then conclude with me that dumb unfeeling mustard has more wit and intelligence than a talking unfeeling fool, as you are."

Some were pleased by the jest, and some were not, but all Tarlton cared about — for his resolution was always this before he talked any jest — was to get a laugh.

43. How Tarlton Took [Smoked] Tobacco at the First Coming up of It.

Tarlton (as did other gentlemen) at the first coming up of tobacco, smoked it more for fashion's sake than otherwise, and being in a room, sitting between two men overcome with wine, and they never seeing the like, wondered at it; and seeing the vapor come out of Tarlton's nose, one of them cried out, "Fire, fire," and threw a cup of wine in Tarlton's face.

"Make no more stir," Tarlton said, "the fire is quenched. If the sheriffs come, it will turn to a fine, as the custom is."

Taking another drink, one of the other men said, "Bah, what a stink it makes. I am almost poisoned."

"If it offends," Tarlton said, "let's everyone take a little of the smell, and so the savor will quickly go," but the stink of the tobacco whiffs made them leave, and leave him to pay for all.

Chapter III: Tarlton's Pretty Country Jests.

44. Tarlton's Wit Between a Bird and a Woodcock.

In the city of Gloucester, Mr. Bird of the Queen's Chapel met with Tarlton, who was joyful to meet and greet the other man again, and they went to visit Mr. Bird's friends. Among the rest, Mr. Bird of the Queen's Chapel visited Mr. Woodcock of the College. When they met, many friendly speeches passed between them, among which Mr. Woodcock challenged Mr. Bird about their kinship, and Mr. Woodcock mused that he was of Mr. Bird's affinity, and he never knew it.

"Yes," Mr. Woodcock said, "every Woodcock is a Bird, therefore it must needs be so."

"Lord Sir," Tarlton said, "you are wide of the mark, for although every Woodcock is a Bird, yet every Bird is not a Woodcock."

So Mr. Woodcock like a woodcock bit his lip, and mumbudget was silent.

Notes:

Mr. Bird was a well-known musician.

A woodcock is a proverbially stupid bird.

"To play at mumbudget" means "to be silent."

45. Tarlton's Jest about a Gridiron.

While the Queen's Players stayed in Worcester City to get money, it was Tarlton's custom to sing extempore on themes — topics — given to him. He let it be known that the following day he would do this for themes given to him by the people for whom the Queen's Players were appointed to perform.

Now one fellow of the city among the rest, who seemed quaint of conceit, aka cunning of thought, to lead other youths with his fine wit, gave out that the next day he would give Tarlton a theme that would make him nonplussed. Several of this man's friends, who were acquainted with Tarlton's ability to adlib, expected some rare conceit [humor].

Well, the next day came, and this gallant fellow gave Tarlton his invention in two lines, which was this:

> I think it is a thing unfit,
> To see a gridiron turn the spit.

The people laughed at this, thinking his wit could not be answered, which angered Tarlton exceedingly, and soon with a smile he looked around, when they expected wonders, and he said these lines:

> I think it is a thing unfit:
> To see an ass have any wit.

The people hooted for joy to see the theme-giver dashed, who like a dog with his tail between his legs left the place. But Tarlton got such commendations that he dined with the bailiff that night, where the theme-giver dared not come, although he was sent for, so much was he vexed at that unlooked-for answer.

46. Tarlton's Answer in Defense of His Flat Nose.

I remember I was once at a play in the country, where Tarlton's custom was, the play being done, everyone who so pleased could throw up to him a written theme to adlib about. Among all the rest, one was read to this effect, word by word:

> Tarlton, I am one of thy friends, and none of thy foes.
> Then I ask you to please tell how you came by thy flat nose:
> Had I been present at that time on those banks,
> I would have laid my short sword over his long shanks.

Tarlton, mad at this question, as it was his character sooner to take such a matter ill than well, very suddenly returned him this answer:

Friend or foe, if thou will needs [necessarily] know,
Mark [listen to] me well [carefully],
With parting dogs and bears, then by the ears,
This chance fell [event happened].
But what of that?
Though my nose is flat,
My credit [reputation] to save,
Yet very well, I can by the smell,
Scent [Distinguish] an honest man from a knave.

Notes:

Tarlton's "friend" seems to think that Tarlton's nose was flattened in a fight.

Tarlton separated dogs and bears at a bear-baiting.

"To set by the ears" is an idiom for "to fight" or "to argue."

Tarlton seems to have gotten his nose busted and flattened at a bear-baiting. The nose-flattening may have been done by accident by someone who helped him separate the dogs and bear, or perhaps one of the animals flattened his nose.

47. Tarlton's Jest about a Bristow Man.

When the Queen's Players were restrained [from playing in London] one summer, they travelled down to Saint James' Fair at Bristow, where Londoners and the Bristow citizens worthily entertained them.

It happened that a wealthy citizen named Mr. Sunbanke one morning secretly married his maid, but the marriage was not so secret, for news of it was blown abroad and it was gossiped about. That morning Tarlton and others walking in the fair to visit his good friends of London, and being in company of Bristow men, they saw Mr. Sunbanke coming, who had the habit of not moving his neck in any way but instead would turn his entire body.

It chanced to happen at the end of the fair, he stood to piss against a wall. Tarlton came over to him, and clapping him on the shoulder, said, "May God give you joy in your marriage."

Mr. Sunbanke, being taken pissing against the wall, wanted to look back to thank him, so suddenly he turned about his entire body and all in the view of many, and showed his penis, which so abashed him that, ashamed, he went into a tavern, protesting that he had rather have spent ten pounds than to have exposed himself.

"Surely," the vintner said, "the fault is in your neck, which will not turn without the body's assistance, and not in Mr. Tarlton."

"Call you him Mr. Tarlton?" Mr. Sunbanke asked.

"Yes, Sir," the vintner said. "He is the Queen's Jester."

"He may be whose jester he will be, but at this time this jest agrees not with me," Mr. Sunbanke said.

48. A Jest Made to Tarlton by a Country Gentleman.

In the country where the Queen's Players were accepted into a gentleman's house, the wagon being unloaded of the apparel and costumes, the wagoner went to Tarlton, and asked him to speak to the steward for provisions for the horses.

"I will," Tarlton said, and coming to the steward, he asked, "Sir, where shall our horses spend the time?"

The gentleman, looking at Tarlton at that question, suddenly answered, "If it please you, or them, let them walk a turn or two, for there is a fair garden, so let them play a game or two of bowling in the alley," and then departed and went about his other business.

Tarlton, commending the quick wit of the steward, said little.

But the steward was not quiet and related to the gentlewomen above at a window how he had driven Tarlton to a nonplus with a jest, whereat they all laughed heartily, at which a serving man who well respected Tarlton ran to him and told him as much.

Tarlton, to add fuel to the fire, and loath to rest thus put off with a jest, went and put the horses in the garden, and turned them out into the bowling alley, which with their heels the horses made havoc. Bowling was the gentleman's favorite pastime.

The ladies, looking out above from a window and seeing horses in the garden alley, called the gentleman, who was a knight, and who then cried out to Tarlton, "Fellow, what do you mean by this?"

"Nothing, sir," Tarlton said, "but two of my horses are at seven up, for a peck of provender, a foolish match that I made. Now they are playing at bowling. Run, run — your steward may come after and cry, 'Rub, rub.'"

Although they smiled at this, yet the steward had no thanks for his labor in setting the horses to such an exercise, and they could not blame Tarlton, who did only as he was bidden.

But because of this jest, the horses had oats and hay, stable room, and everything in plenty.

Notes:

"Seven up" appears to be a game. The first entry for "seven-up" in the OED is for 1830: "The game of all-fours when played for seven 'chalks.'" The earliest OED entry for "all fours" as a card game is 1674. "All fours" meaning a human on all fours was current usage in the age of Tarlton.

According to the OED, "rub" is a now obsolete term that was current in 1613 for "the action of taking all the cards of one suit."

A rub is also an uneven place on the ground that interferes with the movement of a ball used in bowling. Certainly the horses' hooves created rubs that the steward would have to fix.

According to the OED, "chalk" means "A mark, line, or 'score' made with chalk."

The "foolish match" Tarlton made was perhaps matching wits with the steward.

49. How Tarlton Made One of His Company Utterly Forswear Drunkenness.

At Salisbury, Tarlton and his fellows were to play before the mayor and his brethren, but a member of Tarlton's company — a young man — was so drunk that he could not perform. Therefore, Tarlton, as madly angry as the young man was madly drunk, clapped on the young man's legs a huge pair of bolts, aka fetters. The fellow, who was deeply asleep, felt nothing.

When all this was done, they conveyed him to the jail on a man's back, and entreated the jailer to do God good service, and let him lie there until he woke up. While they were about their sport, the fellow awakened, and finding himself imprisoned, and the jail hung round with bolts and shackles, he began to bless himself, and he thought that surely in his drunkenness he had done some crime.

With that he called to know what crime he had been charged with, but no one came to him, and then he thought truly that his crime was capital, and that he was a closely guarded prisoner.

By and by came the jail keeper, who mourned that one so young should come to so shameful a death as hanging. Soon another man came, and then another man doing the same thing as the jail keeper, which further put the young man in a puzzle.

But at last came Tarlton, and others, entreating the jail keeper and asking whether it might yet be possible for them to see their fellow before they went. They very vigorously entreated the jail keeper to let them see the drunken young man.

At length the poor drunken young man called out for them, and in they came.

"Oh, Tom," Tarlton said, "hard was your crime. In your drunkenness you murdered an honest man, and it goes hard for us, too, to have it reported that any of our company is to be hanged for this murder."

"Oh, God! Oh, God!" the fellow said. "Is my crime so great? Then commend me to all my friends."

Well, to make this a short tale, the fellow forswore drunkenness, if he could escape, and by as cunning a wile (to his thinking) they got him out of prison by an "escape," and sent him to London before the rest of the company, and he was not a little glad to be gone.

But see what this jest wrought: By little and little, the fellow stopped his excessive drinking and in time altered his desire for drunkenness and instead stayed sober.

Note:

A bolt is a fetter.

50. How Tarlton Saved His Head from Being Cut Off.

Tarlton once visited the country and lodged in a plain and simple inn, during which time a gentleman, somewhat frantic and distraught of his wits, was dwelling in the same town. With his sword drawn, this madman suddenly rushed into Tarlton's bedchamber. Finding him there in bed, the madman would have slain him, saying, "Villain, would it not be valiantly done if I strike off thy knave's head at one blow?"

Tarlton answered, "Tut, sir, that's nothing to your worship to do. You can as easily strike off two heads at one blow, as one; therefore, if you please, I'll go down and call up another person, and so you may strike off both our heads at once."

The madman believed him and let him slip away.

51. How Tarlton Escaped Imprisonment.

Tarlton had been blustering and swaggering very late one night with two of his friends. As they were coming homewards along Cheapside, the watch being then set, the constable asked, "Who goes there?"

"Three merry men," Tarlton said.

"That answer is not sufficient. Who are you?" the constable asked.

"Why," says Tarlton, "one of us is an eye-maker, and the other is a light-maker."

"What are you saying, knave? Are you mocking me? You said gun one is an eye-maker and the other is a light-maker, but these two properties belong to God only," the constable said.

He then ordered, "Arrest these blasphemers."

"Nay, I request you, good Mr. Constable, to be good in your office," Tarlton said. "I will prove that what I have said is true."

"If you can," the constable said, "you shall pass, otherwise you shall all three be punished."

"Why," Tarlton said, "this fellow is an eye-maker because he is a spectacle-maker; and this other fellow is a maker of light, because he is a chandler and makes and sells candles that make your darkest night as light as your lantern."

The constable, seeing them so pleasant, was well contented. The rest of the watchmen laughed, and Tarlton with his two companions went home quietly.

52. How Tarlton Deceived a Country Wench.

The Queen's Players traveled into the west country to play, and they lodged in a little village some ten miles from Bristow. In this village dwelt a pretty nut-brown lass, to whom Tarlton made an offer of marriage, saying that he had come from London for the purpose of marrying her. The simple maiden being proud to be beloved by such a one whom she knew to be the Queen's man, without more entreaty yielded her body to him. They then went to the church together, where the parson was ready to perform his duty. When the parson came to the words of "I, Richard Tarlton, take thee, Joan," Tarlton said, "Wait, good Master Parson, I will go and call my fellows, and come back to you."

So going out of the church in haste, he returned at leisure; for, having his horse already saddled, he rode toward Bristow, and along the way he told his fellows about his sexual success with this wench.

53. How Tarlton Went to Kill Crows.

It once happened that as Tarlton went forth with a birding gun into the fields to kill crows, he spied a daw sitting in a tree, at which he meant to shoot; but at the same instant, there came a person by, to whom he spoke in this manner: "Sir," he said, "yonder I see a daw, which I will shoot at if she sit."

"If she sit," said the other, "then she is a daw indeed."

"But," Tarlton said, "if she does not sit, what is she then?"

"Indeed," the other said, "she is a daw also."

At these words the daw immediately flew away, whereupon Tarlton spoke merrily in a rhyme, as follows:

> Whether a daw sit, or whether a daw fly,
> Whether a daw stand, or whether a daw lie,
> Whether a daw creep, or whether a daw cry,
> In what case soever a daw persever,
> A daw is a daw, and a daw shall be ever.

Note:
A jackdaw is a small crow with a grey head.

54. How a Poor Beggar Overreached [Got the Better of] Tarlton by Use of His Wit.

As Tarlton one day sat at his own door, a poor old man came to him and begged a penny for the Lord's sake, whereupon Tarlton, having no coins that small about him, asked the beggar, "What money do you have?"

"No more money, mister," the beggar said, "other than one single penny."

Tarlton, being merrily disposed, called for his penny, and having received it, gave it to his boy to fetch a pot of ale: whereat the beggar grew blank [pale], and began to gather up his wits and think about how to get his penny again.

The pot of ale, with the beggar's penny, being brought, Tarlton said that he would drink to the beggar.

"No, wait awhile, mister," the beggar said, "the custom is, where I was born, that he who pays for the drink, must drink first."

"Thou spoke well," Tarlton said. "Go to, and drink to me then."

Whereupon the beggar took the pot, saying, "Here, mister, I drink to you," and then he drank every drop.

The beggar said, "Now, mister, if you will pledge me, send for it as I have done."

Tarlton seeing himself so overreached and outwitted, greatly commended the beggar's wit and intelligence, and withal in recompense thereof, gave him a teaster, aka sixpence.

After receiving the money, the beggar said that he would most truly pray to God for him.

"No," answered Tarlton, "I request that you pray for yourself, for I will take no usury for alms-deeds — that is, for doing a good deed."

55. Of Tarlton's Pleasant Answer to a Gallant by the Highway Side.

It was Tarlton's occasion on another time to ride into Suffolk, being furnished with a very lean large horse, and by the way, a lusty gallant met him and in mockery asked him, "What is a yard of your horse worth?"

"Indeed, sir," Tarlton said, "I ask you to get down from your horse, and lift up my horse's tail, and they in that shop will tell you the price of a yard."

Note:

The word "lusty" can mean "healthy" and "vigorous.

56. How Tarlton Would have Drowned His Wife.

Once, as Tarlton and his wife came sailing as passengers from Southampton towards London, a mighty storm arose, and endangered the ship, whereupon the captain ordered every man to throw into the seas the heaviest thing he could best spare, for the purpose of lightening somewhat the ship. Tarlton pretended to try to throw his wife overboard, but the company rescued her and asked Tarlton, "Why did you want to throw your wife overboard?"

He answered, "She is the heaviest thing I have, and I can best spare her."

57. How Tarlton Made his Will and Testament.

Recently a gentleman living in England, wheresoever he dined, would of every dish convey a modicum thereof into his gown sleeve. This gentleman being once at dinner at a gentleman's house in the country, there he did his accustomed action in the presence of Mr. Tarlton, who perceiving it, said to the company, "My companions, I am now determined before you all, to make my last Will and Testament. And first, I bequeath my soul to God my Creator, and my body to be buried in the sleeve of yonder gentleman's gown."

After saying that, Tarlton stepped over to the gentleman and turned up the gown sleeve, and here dropped out a bit, and there a bit, with choice of much other good food.

Still shaking the sleeve, Tarlton said, "I meant this sleeve, gentleman, this sleeve I meant."

58. How Tarlton Called a Gentleman "Knave" by Craft.

A while afterward, as the same gentleman and Tarlton passed through a field together, a crow in a tree cried, "Kaw, Kaw."

"Look yonder, Tarlton," the gentleman said. "Yonder crow is calling you a knave."

"No, sir," Tarlton answered, "he beckons to your worship as the better man."

59. Tarlton's Jest about a Country Wench.

As Tarlton was going towards Hogsdon, he met a country maiden coming to market. Her mare stumbled, and down she fell, tumbling over and over, showing all that God ever gave her, and then rising up again, she turned to Mr. Tarlton and asked, "By God's body, sir, did you ever see the like before?"

"No, truly," Tarlton replied, "never but once in London."

60. How Tarlton Deceived an Innholder at Sandwich.

Once, when the Queen's Players were put to silence and could not perform, Tarlton and his serving boy frolicked so long in the country that all their money was gone, and being a great way from London, they didn't know what to do, but as want is the whetstone of wit, Tarlton gathered his wits together, and practiced a trick to bear him up to London without money.

They went to an inn in Sandwich, and there lay for two days at great expense, although he had no money to pay for the same. The third morning he told his serving boy to go down and pretend to be malcontent before his host and his hostess, and mumbling say to himself, "Lord, Lord, what a mean, shabby master I serve. This is what it is to serve such seminary priests and Jesuits. Now even as I am an honest boy, I'll leave him in the lurch, and shift for myself. Here's ado about penance and mortification, as though — forsooth — Christ has not died enough for all."

The serving boy mumbled out what Tarlton had instructed him to say so convincingly that it struck a suspicion in the innholder's heart, that no doubt Tarlton was a seminary priest, whereupon the innholder immediately sent for the constable, and told him all the foresaid matter and so they both together went up to arrest Tarlton in his chamber, who purposely had shut himself close in, and betaken himself to his knees, and to his crosses, to make the matter seem more suspicious. The innholder and the constable seeing this through the keyhole, made no more ado, but in they rushed, and arrested him for being a seminary priest, discharged his debt, bore his and his boy's charges up to London, and there in hope to have rich rewards, presented him to Mr. Fleetwood, the old Recorder of London.

But now see how the jest played out:

When the Recorder saw Tarlton, he recognized him very well and entertained him very courteously. Tarlton had completely fooled the innholder and his mate, who were sent away with fleas in their ears, and when Tarlton saw himself discharged out of their hand he stood jesting and pointing at their folly, and so taught them by his cunning to have more wit and thrift in preparation for another time.

Note:

"Forsooth" means "truly" or "indeed."

"To send away with fleas in their ear" means "to send away with sharp, stinging rebukes."

61. Of Tarlton's Wrongful Accusation.

Tarlton was once wrongfully accused of getting a gentleman's maid pregnant and for this offense, he was brought before a justice in Kent. The justice said, "It is a marvel, Mr. Tarlton, that you being a gentleman of good quality, and one of her Majesty's servants, would venture thus to get a maid pregnant.

"No," Tarlton replied, "rather it would be a marvel if a maid had gotten me pregnant."

62. Tarlton Deceived by a Country Wench.

Traveling to play abroad, Tarlton was in a town where in the inn was a pretty maid, whose favor was placed in a corner of Tarlton's affection, and after he talked with her, she promised to meet him at the bottom of a pair of stairs. Night and the hour came, and the maid cunningly sent down her mistress, to whom Tarlton said after catching her in his arms, "Have you come, wench?"

"Oh! Alas!" the mistress said, not knowing who it was.

Tarlton, hearing it was the mistress, jumped aside, and the maid came down with a candle, and she caught a glimpse of Tarlton in the dark as he stepped into another room.

"What is the matter, mistress?" the maid asked.

"Something frightened me," she answered. It was some man, I am sure, for I heard him speak."

"No, no, mistress," the maid said. "It is no man. It was a bullcalf that I shut into a room until John our impounder came to have impounded him as a stray."

"Had I known that," the mistress said, "I would have hit him such a knock on his forehead, that his horns should never have graced his coxcomb," and then she departed, but she was still afraid.

But think about how Tarlton took this jest.

Notes:

In this context, a mistress is a female boss, aka the female head of the inn.

At the time, "wench" could be an endearing term. It was not necessarily negative.

63. How Tarlton Could Not Abide a Cat, and Deceived Himself.

In the country Tarlton told his hostess that he was a conjuror.

"Oh, sir," she said. "I had pewter stolen off my shelf the other day. Help me to get it back, and I will forgive you all the pots of ale you owe me, which is sixteen dozen."

Tarlton replied, "Tomorrow morning the Devil shall help you to get it back, or I will trounce him."

Morning came, and the hostess and he met in a room by themselves. Tarlton, to pass the time with exercise of his wit, attempted to conjure with circles and tricks, but he had no more skill than a dog.

But see how contrarily the jest fell out:

As he was calling out, "Mons, pons, simul, and sons," and similar words, a cat unexpectedly leapt from the gutter window, which sight so amazed Tarlton that he leapt away and knocked his hostess down, so that he departed with his fellows, and left her with her hip out of joint. She put herself in the surgeon's hands and did not dare to tell how she had gotten her injury.

64. How Tarlton and His Hostess of Waltham Met.

Tarlton, riding with several citizens who were his friends to make merry at Waltham, met along the way with his hostess, who was riding toward London, whom he saluted because of their old acquaintance.

She asked, "Where are you going?"

Tarlton told her, "We are going to make merry at Waltham."

"Sir," she replied, "then let me request your company at my house — the Christopher — and for the sake of old acquaintance and friendship, you shall spend your money there."

"Not unless you go back," Tarlton said. "If you don't go back, we will go to the Hound and spend our money there."

Because she was loath to lose their custom, she sent her serving man to London to take care of her business, and she went back with them. As they traveled together, they enjoyed much mirth, for she was an exceedingly merry honest and chaste woman, yet the rumor was that she would take anything, aka that she was promiscuous.

Hearing that she would take anything, Tarlton, as wise as he was, was deceived in his mind when he believed that. Nevertheless, he asked her if the biggest bed in her house were able to hold two of their bigness (meaning himself and her).

"Yes," she said, "and they can tumble up and down at their pleasure."

"Really, with one upon the other?" Tarlton asked.

"And with one under the other, too," she said.

Well, to have their custom and their money, she agreed to everything, like a tricky hostess, and it happened that Tarlton, having her in a room at her house, asked her, "Which of those two beds is big enough for us two?"

"This one," she said. "Therefore, go to bed, sweetheart, and I'll come to you."

"By the mass," Tarlton said, "if my boots were off, I would indeed."

"I'll help you, sir," she said, "if you please."

I see, Tarlton thought. *Is the wind in that door?*

He said to her, "Come on then."

And she very diligently began to pull, and she pulled until one boot was half off.

"Now," she said, "this being hard to do, let me try my skill on the other, and so get off both."

But having pulled both boots half off his legs, she left him alone in the shoemaker's stocks, and she — still honest and chaste — went to London.

Tarlton was in the shoemaker's stocks for three hours, and he had no help.

But eventually being eased of his pain, he made this rhyme for a theme, and he sang it all the way to London:

> Women are wanton, and hold it no sin,
> By tricks and devices to pull a man in.

Notes:

"To take anyone" means to have sex with anyone.

According to the OED, "is the wind in that door?" means "is the wind in that quarter?" or "is that the tendency of affairs?"

65. Tarlton's Meeting with his Country Acquaintance at Ilford.

One Sunday, Tarlton rode to Ilford, where his father stayed, and while he was dining with him at his sister's, there came in several people of the country to see him, amongst whom was one plain country plow-jogger, aka plowman, who said he was of Tarlton's kin, and so called him "cousin."

Tarlton asked his father, "Is this true? Are he and I related?"

But his father knew no such thing.

Hearing this, Tarlton said, "Whether he is of my kin or not, I will be his cousin before we part, if all the drink in Ilford will do it."

So they caroused freely, and the clown was then in his cue so that (in brief) they were both in soundly. In other words, they both partied, they were friends, and they got thoroughly drunk.

Night came and Tarlton would not let his "cousin" go, but said that they would lie together in the same bed that night, meaning to have a drink at their departure next morning.

Tarlton would by wit leave him in the lash, since power would not. But see the jest:

That night the plain fellow so pissed on Tarlton in his bed, thinking he was pissing against the church wall, that Tarlton was obliged to cry for a fresh shirt to change into.

So when all was well, they must necessarily drink at parting. Where indeed (to seal their kindredship soundly) the fellow had his load, aka drank his fill.

For hearing that his cousin Tarlton had gone to London, the country fellow said that by God's wounds he would follow Tarlton, that he would, and none could hold him, and meaning to go towards London, his aim was so "good" that he went towards Rumford to sell his hogs.

Notes:

The word "cousin" at the time meant "relative," not "cousin" as we understand it.

The word "clown" means 1) countryman or rustic fellow, and 2) jester and professional fool.

In this society, it was not uncommon for two unmarried people of the same sex to share a bed. No homosexuality is implied.

According to the OED, "to leave in the lash" may mean "to leave in the lurch." Also, "to run in or upon the lash" may mean "to incur more debts than one can pay."

"To leave in the lash" means to leave "in the dirt, mud, or lurch," according to James Orchard Halliwell, *A Dictionary of Archaic and Provincial Words*, 1847.

Most likely, Tarlton simply meant to leave the plowman in Ilford without playing a trick on him, but here are two other possibilities:

1) Possibly, Tarlton was planning to leave early, not have a parting drink with his "cousin," and stick him with the bill.

2) Also possibly, Tarlton was trying to resort to this sort of trick due to not being able to get rid of his "cousin." Since he lacked the

power to get rid of him, he would use his wit, aka intelligence, and try to trick him by drinking a lot and then leaving him with the bill. If so, the trick didn't work because the fellow in his sleep pissed on Tarlton, who cried out and woke the fellow up.

As things turned out, it seems that they parted on fairly good terms. Apparently, the fellow kept on drinking after Tarlton left.

66. How a Maid Drove Tarlton to be Nonplussed.

Tarlton met a wily country wench who gave him quip for quip.

"Sweetheart," he said, "I wish that my flesh were in your flesh."

"So wish I, sir," she said. "I wish your nose were in my I-know-where."

Tarlton, angered at this, said no more, but went on his way.

Notes:

Obviously, sexual harassment was present in the late 1500s, but so were snappy comebacks to harassing comments.

The wench's "I-know-where" is the stinkiest part of her body.

67. Tarlton's Answer to a Question.

Someone asked Tarlton, "Why is Monday called Sunday's fellow?"

"Because he is a saucy fellow," Tarlton said, "to compare himself with that holy day. But it may be that Monday thinks himself Sunday's fellow because it follows Sunday and is the next day after Sunday, but it comes a day after the fair for all that."

"But if two Sundays should fall together," the fellow said, "Monday then may be the first, and it would show well, too."

"Yes," Tarlton said, "but if your nose stood under your mouth, it would show better, and be more for your profit."

"How could it be more for my profit?" the fellow asked.

"Indeed," Tarlton said, "it would never be cold in winter, being so near every dog's tail."

The fellow, seeing that a foolish question had a foolish answer, laid his legs on his neck, and got him gone.

Notes:

According to the OED, "(to come) a day after the fair" means "(to arrive or occur) too late."

According to *Dictionary of Proverbs* by George Latimer Apperson and Martin H. Manser, "to lay one's legs on one's neck" means "to be off." They cite *Tarlton's Jests* in support. It is possible, however, that the phrase is meant to be ridiculous and have no real meaning. I agree that "to lay one's legs on the ground" means to leave hastily.

If the person's nose were under his mouth, and his mouth were to swallow every dog's tail, the person's nose would be close to the dog's anus, which would be a source of heat.

Can "being so near every dog's tail" be a reference to fellatio?

It is possible, of course, that Tarlton's answer is simply meant to be ridiculous.

68. Tarlton's Desire to Get a Good Deal on Oats for His Money.

Tarlton, coming into a market town, bought oats for his horse, and desired a good deal on oats for his money.

The man said, "You shall have it, sir," and gave him two half pecks of oats for the money that would usually buy one half peck of oats.

Tarlton thought his horse should eat well that night, and so he went to his horse and recited this rhyme:

Jack Nag, swagger, and lustfully enjoy it,
I have enough oats for my money, and you shall have it.

But when Jack Nag smelled the oats, they were so musty that he would not eat them. ("May God thank you, master, but no oats for me.")

Seeing this, Tarlton ran into the marketplace and wanted to slash and cut the fellow. But until the next market day, the fellow was not to be found, and before then Tarlton had to be gone.

69. How Tarlton's Dog Licked up Six Pence.

Tarlton in his travels had a dog of fine qualities. Among the rest of his fine tricks, the dog would carry six pence at the end of his tongue.

Tarlton would brag often about this trick, and say, "Never was the like of this dog."

"Yes, there is," a lady said. "My dog is more strange, for he will bear a French crown in his mouth."

"No," Tarlton said, "I think not."

"Lend me a French crown," the lady said, "and you shall see."

Tarlton replied, "Truly, madam, I don't have it, but if your dog will carry a cracked English crown, here it is."

The lady did not perceive the jest, but she was desirous to see the dog's trick with six pence. Tarlton threw down a six-pence piece, and said to his dog, "Bring it to me, sirrah."

It was just his luck that the dog took up a brass counter, and let the money lie on the floor.

A gentlewoman nearby, seeing that, asked Tarlton, "How long will the dog hold it?"

"An hour," Tarlton said.

"That is a pretty neat trick," the gentlewoman said. "Let's see that."

In the meantime she picked up the sixpence, and then she asked him to let them see the money again. When he got the "money" from his dog, he saw that it was a brass counter, and he made this rhyme:

> Alas, alas, how came all this to pass?
> The world's worse than it was:
> For silver turns to brass.

"Aye," said the lady, "and the dog has made its master an ass."

Tarlton would never trust to his dog's tricks anymore.

Notes:

A cracked English crown is the injured head of an English person.

According to OED (first entry 1610), "cracked" can mean "Of the brain, mind, etc.: Unsound, impaired, somewhat deranged. Of a person: Unsound in mind, slightly insane, crazy." This seems applicable to Tarlton and his brain.

Of course, a crown is a unit of English money.

A brass counter is a brass piece of circular metal that is an imitation of real money. It is a token.

70. Tarlton's Jest about a Horse and a Man.

In the city of Norwich, Tarlton was invited to a hunt where there was a goodly gentlewoman, who bravely mounted on a black horse and rode exceedingly well, to the wonder of all the beholders, and neither hedge nor ditch stood in her way, but Pegasus her horse (for so we may name him because of his swiftness) flew over all, and she sat on him as well as he flew.

When everyone returned home, at supper some commended the host's hound, others commended the host's hawk, and she above all commended her host's horse that she had ridden, saying, "I love no living creature as well — at this instant — as I love my gallant horse."

"Yes, lady, you love a man better," Tarlton said.

"Indeed, no," she said. "Not now. For since my last husband died, I hate men most, unless you can give me medicines to make me love them."

Tarlton made this jest instantly:

> Why, a horse mingeth whay, Madam, and a man mingeth amber,
> A horse is for your way, Madam, but a man is for your chamber.

In other words:

> Why, a horse urinates whey, Madam, a man urinates amber,

> A horse is for you to ride on your way, Madam, but a man is for you to ride in your bedchamber.

"God-a-mercy, Tarlton," the men present said.

The phrase "God-a-mercy" expressed applause.

The gentlewoman, hearing this and seeing that they took exception at her words, answered thus to make all well:

> That a horse is chief in my opinion now, I deny not,
> And when a man does me more good in my bedchamber, I
> him defy not.
> But until then give me leave [permission] to love something.

"Then some thing will please you," Tarlton said. "I am glad of that; therefore, I pray that God sends you a good thing, or none at all."

Notes:

At the time "whay" could be used to pun on "way or path" and "whoa," as well as on the watery part of milk left after the curd has coagulated and been removed.

A "thing" can be a penis.

71. Tarlton's Talk with a Pretty Woman.

"Gentlewoman," Tarlton said, "and the rest of you as you sit, I can tell you strange things."

Many gallants at supper had noticed this one gentlewoman who was little and pretty, but unfortunately had a large, wide mouth that lessened her prettiness.

She, attempting to hide her large, wide mouth, would pinch in her speeches, and speak softly, but she wanted to hear Tarlton's news.

Tarlton said that as he traveled to Norwich, he had heard that a proclamation was made in London that every man should have two wives.

"Now, by Jesus," she said, "is it possible?"

"Aye, gentlewoman, and it is able, too, for contrarily women will have a larger preeminence, for every woman must have three husbands."

"Now, Jawsus," said the gentlewoman, and with her wonder she showed the full wideness of her mouth, which all the people at the table smiled at.

Perceiving this, the gentlewoman would say no more.

"Now, mistress," Tarlton said, "your mouth is less than it ever was, for now it is able to say nothing."

"You are a cheating knave," she said.

"By the mass, and that is something yet," Tarlton said, "your mouth shall be as wide as ever it was, on account of that jest."

Note:

"Jawsus" may be used rather than "Jesus" in order to make a reference to the woman's jaw.

72. A Jest by Tarlton to a Great, Huge Man.

A great, huge man, three yards in the waist, was at St. Edmondsbury in Suffolk. (He died only recently.) He was named Mr. Blague, and he was a good kind justice, too, for he helped the poor.

This justice met with Tarlton in Norwich and said, "Tarlton, give me your hand."

"But, you, sir, being richer, may give me a greater gift," Tarlton said. "Give me your body."

Embracing him, Tarlton could not half encircle him.

Being merry in talk, the justice said, "Tarlton, tell me one thing: What is the difference between a flea and a louse?"

"Indeed, sir," Tarlton said, "There is as much and as like difference as between you and me. I, like a flea, as you can see" — he skipped — "can skip nimbly.

"But you, like a fat louse, creep slowly, and you can go no faster, even if butchers were over you, ready to knock you on the head."

"You are a knave," the justice said.

"Aye, sir," Tarlton said. "I knew that before I came hither, else I had not been here now, for always one knave" — he paused — "seeks out another."

Understanding him, the justice laughed heartily.

73. Tarlton's Jest to a Maid in the Dark.

Tarlton, going in the dark, groped his way and heard the tread of someone coming toward him.

"Who goes there?" he asked. "A man, or a monster?"

A maiden answered, "A monster."

Tarlton said, "A candle hoe."

Seeing the maiden, he said, "Indeed, it's a monster, I'll be sworn, for your teeth are longer than your head."

"Oh, sir," the maiden said, "speak no more than you see, for women go about invisible nowadays."

Notes:

My guess is that a candle hoe is a candleholder.

According to the OED, a then-current meaning of "hoe' is "Care, anxiety, trouble."

A candle-hour is an hour in which candles are burned — that is, an hour of nighttime.

According to the OED, in the years circa 1000 through 1300, "ho" meant "heel." "Candle ho" may mean candle stub.

74. Tarlton's Jest to a Dog.

Tarlton and his fellows, being in the Bishop of Worcester's wine cellar, and being largely laid to, Tarlton had his rouse, and as he went through the streets, a dog lying in the middle of the street, asleep on a dunghill, suddenly barked because Tarlton reeled on him.

"How are you now, dog?" Tarlton asked. "Are you in your humors?"

And for many days afterward, it was a byword to describe a drunken man to say that he was in his humors.

Notes:

"Laid to" means "cast down from an erect position" (OED). Tarlton is so drunk that he has a hard time standing upright.

"Rouse" means a large vessel of wine, or a drinking bout.

"Humors" are moods or dispositions.

APPENDIX A: TARLTON'S JESTS (THE ORIGINAL)

***Tarltons* Court-Witty Iests.**

How *Tarlton* plaid the Drunkard before the Queene.

1. THE Quéene being discontented; which *Tarlton* perceiuing, took vp|on him to delight her with some quaint iest: whereupon he counter|faited a drunkard, and called for Béere, which was brought immedi|ately. Her Maiestie noting his hu|mor, commanded that he should haue no more: for (quoth shée) he will play the beast, and so shame himselfe. Feare not you (quoth *Tarlton*) for your Béere is small enough. Whereat her Maiestie laughed heartily, and commanded that he should haue enough.

2. **How *Tarlton* deceiued the Watch in Fleetstreet.**

TArlton hauing bin late at Court, & cōming home|wards thorow Fléetstréet, he espied the Watch, and not knowing how to passe them, hée went very fast, thinking by that meanes to goe vnexmained: But the Watchmen perceiuing that hee shunned them, stept to him, & commanded him in the Queenes name to stand. Stand, quoth *Tarlton?* let them stand that can, for I can|not. So falling downe, as though he had been drunke, they helpt him vp, and so let him passe.

3. **How *Tarlton* flowted a Lady in the Court.**

VPon a time, *Tarlton* being among certaine Ladies at a banquet which was at *Greenewich,* the Quéene then lying there, one of the Ladies had her face ful of pim|ples with heat at her stomake, for which cause she refused to drinke wine amongst the rest of the Ladies: which *Tarl*|*ton*perceiuing (for he was there of purpose to iest amongst them) quoth he, A marren of that face, which makes all the body fare the worse for it. At which the rest of the Ladies laught, and she (blushing for shame) left the banquet.

4. ***Tarltons* opinion of Oysters.**

CErtaine Noblemen and Ladies of the Court, being eating of Oysters, one of them séeing *Tarlton,* called him, & asked him if he loued Oysters? No (quoth *Tarlton*) for they be vngodly meate, vncharitable meat, and vnpro|fitable meate. Why, quoth the Courtiers; They are vn|godly, sayes *Tarlton,* because they are eaten without grace, vncharitable, because they leaue nought but shelles: and vnprofitable, because they must swim in wine.

5. *Tarltons* resolution of a question

ONe of the company taking the Gentlemans part, as|ked *Tarlton* at what time he thought the Diuell to be most busied? When the Pope dies, (quoth he.) Why saies the Courtier? Marry (answered he) then all the Deuils are troubled and busied to plague him: for he hath sent many a soule before him thither, that exclaime against him.

6. How a parsonage fell into *Tarltons* hands.

HEr Maiestie dining in the *Strand* at the Lord Trea|surers, the Lords were very desirous that she would vouchsafe to stay all night: but nothing could preuaile with her. *Tarlton* was in his Clownes apparell, being all dinner while in the presence with her, to make her merry: and hea|ring the sorrow that the Noblemen made, that they could not worke her stay: he asked the Nobles what they would giue him to worke her stay? The Lords promised him any thing, to performe it. Quoth he Procure me the Parsonage of *Shard.* They caused the patent to be drawne presently: he got on a Parsons gowne and a corner-Cap, & standing vpon the staires, where the Quéene should descend, he repeated these words: A Parson, or no Parson? A Parson, or no Parson: but after she knew his meaning, shée not only stayd all night, but the next day willed hée should haue possession of the Benefice. A madder Parson was neuer, for he threatned to turne the Bell-mettle into lyning for his purse: which he did, the Parsonage and all, into ready money.

7. How *Tarlton* Proued two Gentlewomen dishonest by their owne words.

TArlton séeing in Gréenwich two Gentlewomen in the Garden together, to moue mirth comes to them, and enquires thus: Gentlewomen, which of you two is the ho|nester? I, sayes the one, I hope without exceptions: and I quoth the other, since we must speake for our selues: so then sayes *Tarlton,* one of you by your own words is dishonese, one being honester then the other, else you would answere otherwise: but as I found you, so I leaue you.

8. How *Tarlton* answered a wanton Gentlewoman.

A Gentlewoman merrily disposed, being crost by *Tarlton,* and halfe angry, said, Sirra, a little thing would make mée requite you with a cuffe. With a cuff, Lady, sayes *Tarlton*? so would you spell my sorrow forward: but spell my sorrow backward, then cuffe me and spare not when the Gentlemen by considered of the word, they laughing, made the simple-meaning Gentlewoman to blush for shame.

9. How *Tarlton* dared a Lady.

AT the Dinner in the great Chamber where *Tarlton* iested, the Ladies were daring one another: quoth one, I euer durst do any thing that is honest and Honoura|ble. A French crowne of that, sayes *Tarlton.* Ten pound of that sayes the Lady. Done, sayes one, Done sayes another. *Tarlton* put two pence betwixt his lips, and dared her to take it away with her lips. Fie, sayes shée, that is immode|sty. What to kisse, sayes *Tarlton?* then immodesty beares a great hand ouer all: but once in your life say, you haue béene beaten at your owne weapon. Well, Sir, sayes shee, you may say any thing. Then sayes *Tarlton,* remember, I say you dare not, and so my wager is good.

10. How *Tarlton* landed at Cuckolds haven.

TArlton being one Sunday at Court all day, caused a paire of Oares to tend him, who at night called on him to be gone. *Tarlton* being a carousing, drunk so long to the Watermen, that one of them was bumpsie, and so in|déede were all thrée for the most part: at last they left Gréenwich, the Tide being at a great low fall▪ the Water|men yet afraide of the Crosse Cables by the Lime-house, very dark and late as

it was, landed *Tarlton* at Cuckolds-hauen, and said, the next day they
would giue him a reason for it: But *Tarlton* was faine to goe by land
to Redriffe on the dirty banke, euery step knée-déepe: so that cōming
home, hée called one of his boyes to help him off with his boots,
meaning his stockings, which were died of another colour. Whereupon
one gaue him this theame the next day:

> *Tarlton,* tell mee: for fayne would I know,
> If thou wert landed at Cuckholds-haven or no?

Tarlton answered thus:

> Yes, Sir, and I tak't in, no scorne:
> For many land there yet misse of the horne.

11. How *Tarlton* fought with blacke Davie.

NOt long since liued a little swaggerer: called Blacke *Davie,* who
would at Sword and Buckler fight with any Gentleman or other, for
twelue pence: he being hired to draw vpon *Tarlton,* for breaking a iest
vpon huffing *Kate,* a Punke, as men termed her: one euening, *Tarlton*
comming forth at the Court gate, being at Whitehall, and walking
toward the Tilt-yard, this *Davie* immediately drew vpon *Tarlton:* who
on the sudden, though amazed, drew likewise, and enquired the cause:
which *Davie* denied, till they had fought a bout or two. *Tarlton*
couragiously got within him, and taking him in his armes, threw him
into the Tilt-yard, who falling vpon his nose, broke it extreme|ly, that
euer after he snuffled in the head; poore *Dauie* lying all that night in
the Tilt- yard, expecting the doores to be opened came forth, and at
the Barber-surgeons told of this bloody combat: and the occasion of it
was (quoth he) because *Tarlton* being in a Tauerne, in the company of
this-dam|nable Cackatrice, huffing *Kate,* called for wine, but she told
him, That without he would burne it, she would not drink. No quoth
Tarlton, it shall be burnt, for thou canst burne it without fire. As how

Sir (quoth she?) Mary thus. Take the Cup in thine hand, and I will tell thée. So he filling the cup in her hand, said it was burnt sufficiently in so fiery a place: shée perceiuing her selfe so slouted, hired me to be her Champion, to reuenge her quarrell.

12. How *Tarlton* answered the VVatchmen, comming from the Court.

TArlton hauing plaied before the Quéene till one a clock at midnight, comming homewards, one of them espied him, called him, Sirra what art thou? A woman, sayes *Tarlton*. Nay, that is a lye, say the Watchmen; wo|men haue no such beards. *Tarlton* replyed, if I should haue said a man, that you know to be true, and would haue bid|den me, tel you that you know not, therefore I said a wo|man, and so I am all woman, hauing pleased the Quéen, being a woman. Well, sirra, sayes another, I present the Queene: then am I a woman, indeed, sayes *Tarlton,* as well as you, for you haue a beard as well as I, and truly Mistris *Annis,* my buske is not done yet: when will yours? leaue thy gibing, fellow, saith the Watch, the Queenes will is, That whosoeuer is taken without doores after ten a clocke, shall bee committed, and now it is past one: com|mit all such, sayes *Tarlton,* for if it be past one a clocke, it will not be ten this eight houres: with that one lifts vp his Lanthorne, and lookes him in the face, and knew him; In|deed M. *Tarlton* you haue more wit then all we, for it is true, that ten was before one, but now one is before ten. It is true, quoth *Tarlton,* Watch-men had wont to haue more wit, but for want of sléepe they are turned fooles: so *Tarlton* stole from them: and they to séeme wise, went home to bed.

13. *Tarltons* answer to a Courtier.

TArlton being at the Court all night, in the morning he met a great Courtier cōming from his Chamber, who espying *Tarlton,* said: Good morrow, M. *Didimus* and *Tridimus: Tarlton* being somewhat abashed, not know|ing the meaning thereof, said, Sir, I vnderstand you not, expound, I pray you. Quoth the Courtier, *Didimus* and *Tridimus,* is a

foole and a knaue: you ouerloade me, re|plied *Tarlton,* for my backe
cannot beare both; therefore take you the one, and I will take the other,
take you the knaue, and I will carry the foole with me.

14. *Tarltons* quip for a yong Courtier.

THere was a young Gentleman in the Court, that had first lien
with the Mother, and after with the Daugh|ter, and hauing so done,
asked *Tarlton*what it resembled: quoth he, As if you should first haue
eaten the Hen, and af|er, the Chicken.

15. *Tarltons* answere to a Noblemans question.

THere was a Nobleman that asked *Tarlton* what hée thought of
Souldiers in time of Peace. Marry (quoth he) they are like Chimnies in
Summer.

16. *Tarltons* Iest to an vnthrifty Courtier.

THere was an vnthriftie Gallant belonging to the Court, that had
borrowd fiue pounds of *Tarlton:* but hauing lost it at Dice, he sent his
man to *Tarlton* to bor|row fiue pounds more, by the same token hée
owed him already fiue pounds. Pray tel your Master (quoth *Tarlton*)
that if he will send me the token, I will send him the mo|ney: for who
deceiues me once, God forgiue him: if twice, God forgiue him: but if
thrice, God forgiue him, but not me, because I could not beware.

17. How *Tarlton* flouted two Gallants.

TArlton being in a merry vaine, as hée walked in the great Hall in
Greenwitch, hée met my old Lord Chamberlaine, going betwéene two
fantasticke Gallants, and cryed aloud vnto him, my Lord, my Lord, you
goe in great danger: whereat amazed, hée asked whereof: of drowning
(quoth *Tarlton*) were it not for those two blad|ders vnder each of your
armes.

Tarltons sound City Iests.

18. *Tarltons* iest of a red face.

TO an Ordinary in White Fryers, where Gentlemen vsed, by
reason of extraordinary diet, to this *Tarlton* often frequented, as well to
continue acquaintance as to please his ap|petite. It chanced ●o vpon a

time (especially) being set amongst the Gentlemen and Gal|lants, they enquired of him, why melancholy had got the vpper hand of his mirth; to which he said little, but with a squint eye (as custome had made him hare eyed) hée looked for a Iest to make them merry. At last hée espied one that sate on his left side, which had a very red face, he being a very great Gentleman, (which was all one to *Tarlton*) hée presently in great haste called his Host: Who doe I serue (my Host) quoth *Tarlton*; The Quéenes Maiestie, replied the Good man of the house. How happens it then, quoth *Tarlton,* that (to her Maiesties disgrace) you dare make me a companion with Seruingmen, clapping my Lord *Shan|doyes* Cullisance vpon my sléeue, looking at the Gentleman with the red face; mée thinkes, quoth he, it fits like the Saracens head without Newgate. The Gentlemans Sa|lamanders face burnt like *Erna* for anger. The rest laugh|ed heartily. In the end (all enraged) the Gentleman swore to fight with him at next méeting.

19. A sudden and dangerous fray, twixt a Gentleman and *Tarlton,* which he put off with a iest.

AS *Tarlton* and others passed along Fléet-stréet, he espied a spruse yong Gallant, black of complexion, with long haire hanging downe ouer his eares, and his beard of the Italian cut, in white Sattin, very quaintly cut, and his body so stiffely starcht, that he could not bend him|selfe any way for no gold. *Tarlton,* séeing such a wonder comming, trips before him, and méeting this Gallant, tooke the wall of him, knowing that one so proud, at least looked for the prerogatiue. The Gallant scorning that a Player should take the wall, or so much indignifie him, turnes himselfe, and presently drew his Rapier. *Tarlton,* drew likewise. The Gentleman fell to it roundly: but *Tarl|ton* (in his owne defence) compassing and trauersing his ground, gaped with a wide mouth, whereat the people laughed: the Gentleman pausing, enquired why he gaped so, O Sir, saies he, in hope to swallow you; for by my troth you séeme to me like a Prune in a messe of white Broth. At this the people parted them. The Gentleman noting his mad humour, went his way wel contented: for he knew not how to amend it.

20. *Tarltons* Iest of a Pippin.

AT the *Bull* in *Bishops-gate-street,* where the Quéenes Players oftentimes played, *Tarlton* comming on the Stage, one from the Gallery threw a Pippin at him. *Tarl|ton* tooke vp the Pip, and looking on it, made this sudden iest.

> Pip in, or nose in, chuse you whether,
> Put yours in, ere I put in the other.
> Pippin you haue put in: then, for my grace,
> Would I might put your nose in another place.

21. A iest of an Apple hitting *Tarlton* on the face.

TArlton hauing flouted the fellow for his pippin which hée threw, hée thought to beméet with *Tarlton* at length. So in the Play *Tarltons* part was to trauell, who knéeling down to aske his father blessing, the fellow threw an Apple at him, which hit him on the chéek. *Tarlton* ta|king vp the Apple, made this iest.

> Gentleman, this fellow, with this face of Mapple,
> Instead of a pipin, hath throwne me an Apple,
> But as for an Apple, he hath cast a Crab,
> So in stead of an honest woman, God hath sent him a drab.

The people laughed heartily, for he had a Queane to his wife.

22. How *Tarlton* and one in the Gallery fell out.

IT chanced that in the midst of a Play, after long expec|tation for *Tarlton:* being much desired of the people, at length hée came forth: where (at his entrance) one in the Gallerie pointed his finger at him, saying to a friend that had neuer séene him, that is he. *Tarlton* to make sport at the least occasion giuen him, and séeing the man point with the finger, he in loue againe held vp two fingers: the cap|tious fellow, iealous of his wife, (for he was married) and because a Player did it, took the matter more hainously, & asked him why he made hornes at him; No (quoth *Tarl|ton* they be fingers:

> For there is no man, Which in loue to me,
> Lends me one finger, but he shall have three.

No, no, sayes the fellow, you gaue me the hornes. True (sayes *Tarlton*) for my fingers are tipt with nailes, which are like hornes, and I must make a shew of that which you are sure of. This matter grew so, that the more he meddled, the more it was for his disgrace: wherefore the standers by counselled him to depart, both hée and his hornes, lest his cause grew desperate. So the poore fellow, plucking his hat ouer his eyes, went his wayes.

23. How Fiddlers fiddled away *Tarltons* apparell.

IT chanced that one *Fancy* and *Nancy,* two Musicians in London, vsed often with their boyes to visit *Tarlton,* when he dwelt in *Gracious-street*at the signe of the *Saba,* a Tauerne, he being one of their best friends or benefa|ctors, by reason of old acquaintance: to requite which, they came one Summers morning to play him *The Hunt's vp,* with such Musicke as they had. *Tarlton,* to requite them, would open his chamber doore, and for their paines would giue them Muskadine: which a Cony-catcher noting, and séeing *Tarlton* came forth in his shirt and night|gowne to drinke with these Musicians, the while this nimble fellow stept in, and tooke *Tarltons* apparell, which euery day he wore, thinking that if he were espied to turne it to a iest: but it past for currant, and he goes his wayes. Not long after *Tarlton* returned to his chamber, & looked for his cloaths: but they were safe enough from him. The next day this was noised abroad, and one in mockage threw him in this theame, he playing then at the Cur|taine:

> *Tarlton,* I will tell thee a iest,
> Which after turned to earnest:

One there was, as I heard say,
Who in his shirt heard Musicke play,
While all his clothes were stolne away.

Tarlton smiling at this, answered on the sudden thus,

That's certaine, Sir, it is no lie
That same one in truth was I,
When that the theefe shall Pine and lacke,
Then shall I haue cloathes to my backe:
And I, together with my fellowes,
May see them ride to Tiborne Gallowes.

24. Of *Tarlton* and a beggar.

T'There was a poore begger but a conceited fellow, who séeing *Tarlton* at his doore, asked somthing of him for Gods cause. *Tarlton* putting his hand in his pocket, gaue him two pence in stead of a penny: at which *Tarlton* made this Ryme;

Of all the Beggers most happy thou art,
For to thee mine hand is better then my heart.

Quoth the Begger.

True it is, Master, as it chanceth now:
The better for me, and the worse for you.

25. How *Tarlton* deceived a Doctor of Physicke.

TArlton, to satisfie the humours of certaine Gentlemen his familiar acquaintance, went about for to try the skil of a simple Doctor of Physick, that dwelt not far from Islington, and thus it was: he tooke a faire Urinal, and fil|led it halfe full of good Wine, and bore it to this Doctor, saying it was a sick mans water: he viewed it, and tossing it vp and downe, as though he had great knowledge: quoth he, the

Patient whose water it is, is full of grosse humors, and hath néede of purging, and to be let some ten ounces of bloud. No, you Dunce, replyed *Tarlton,* it is good pisse, and with that drunke it off, and threw the Urinall at his head.

26. How *Tarlton* frighted a Country fellow.

TArlton passing through London, by chance he heard a simple Country fellow in an Ale-house, calling for a Kingstone pot of Ale, stept in to him, and threatned to ac|cuse him of treason, saying Sirra, I haue séene and tasted of a penny pot of Ale, and haue found good of the price, but of a Kingstone coyne I neuer heard: therefore it is some counterfet, and I must know how thou camest by it: here|upon, the country fellow was driuen into such a maze, that out of doores he got, and tooke him to his héeles, as though wilde-fire had followed him.

27. How *Tarlton* was deceiued by his Wife in London.

TArlton, being merrily disposed as his Wife and he sate together, he said vnto her, *Kate,* answer me to one que|stion, without a lye, and take this crown of gold: which shée took on condition, that if she lost, to restore it back again. Quoth *Tarlton,* am I a Cuckold or no, *Kate;* Whereat shée answered not a word, but stood silent, notwithstanding he vrged her many waies. *Tarlton* séeing she would not speak, askt his gold againe. Why, quoth shée, haue I made any lye; no, sayes *Tarlton:* why then good man foole, I haue won the wager. *Tarlton* mad with anger, made this Rime.

> As women in speech can reuile a man;
> So can they in silence beguile a man.

28. One askt *Tarlton* what country man the Diuell was.

IN Carter Lane dwelt a merry Cobler, who being in company with *Tarlton,* askt him what Country-man the Diuell was; quoth *Tarlton,* a Spaniard: for Spaniards like the Diuel, trouble the whole world.

29. A Cheese-mongers question to *Tarlton.*

IN time of scarsity, a simple Chéese-monger hearing *Tarlton* commended for his quick wit came vnto him and asked him, why he thought Chéese and Butter to be so ●●●re; *Tarlton* answered, Because Wood and Coales are so ●●●re, for Butter and Chéese a man may eate without a fire.

30. *Tarltons* answere to a rich Londoner.

TArlton méeting a rich Londoner, fell into talke about the Bishop of Peterborough, highly praising his boun|tie to his seruants, his liberality to strangers, his great hospitality and charity to the poore. He doth well, sayes the rich man, for what he hath, he hath but during his life. Why (quoth *Tarlton*) for how many liues haue you your goods?

31. How *Tarlton* gaue away his dinner.

AS *Tarlton* and his wife sate at dinner, his wife being displeased with him, and thinking to crosse him, she gaue away halfe his meat vnto a poore Begger, saying, Take this for my other husbands sake. Whereupon *Tarl|ton* tooke all that was left, and likewise bade the poore fel|low to pray for his other wiues soule.

32. *Tarltons* answere to a boy in a Rime.

THere was a crackrope Boy, méeting *Tarlton* in *Lon|don* stréet, sung this Rime vnto *Tarlton:*

Woe worth thee *Tarlton,*
That euer thou wast borne:
Thy Wife hath made thee Cuckold,
And thou must weare the horne.

Tarlton presently answered him in Extemporie.

What and if I be (Boy)
Ime ne're the worse:
She keepes me like a Gentleman,
With mony in my purse.

33. How *Tarlton* bad himselfe to dinner to my Lord Maiors.

A Iest came in *Tarltons* head where to dine: & thought he, in all that a man does, let him aime at the fairest: for sure if I bid my selfe any where this day, it shall be to my Lords Maiors: and vpon this goes to the Counter, and entered his action against my Lord Maior, who was pre|sently told of it, and sends for him. *Tarlton* waits dinner time, and then comes, who was admitted presently. Master *Tarlton* (saies my Lord Maior) haue you entered an action against me in the Poultry Counter? My Lord (saies *Tarl|ton*) haue you entred an action against mée in Woodstréet Counter? Not I in troth, saies my Lord. No (saies *Tarl|ton*) he was a villaine that told me so then: but if it bée not so, forgiue me this fault, my Lord, and I will neuer offend in the next. But in the end he begins to sweare, how he will be reuenged on him that mockt him, and flings out in a rage. But my Lord said, Stay, M. *Tarlton,* dine with me, and no doubt but after dinner you will be better minded. I will try that, my Lord, saies *Tarlton,* and if it alter mine anger, both mine enemy and I will thanke you together for this courtesie.

34. *Tarltons* Iest of a box on the eare.

ONe that fell out with his friend, méetes him in the stréet, and calling him into a corner, gaue him a box on the eare, and feld him, getting him gone, and neuer told wherefore he did so: which *Tarlton* beholding, raised vp the fellow, and asked him the reason of their suddē falling out. Can you tell, Sir, said the fellow? for by my troth as yet I cannot. Well said *Tarlton,* the more foole you: for had I such féeling of the cause, my wit would remember the iniurie: but many men are goslings; the more they féele, the lesse they conceiue.

35. *Tarltons* Iest to two Tailors.

TArlton méeting two Tailors (friends of his) in the euening in mirth cries, Who goes there, A man, an|swered a Tailor: How many is there? one? Yea, said *Tarlton:* two, said the other Tailor: then you say true, said *Tarlton:* for two Tailors goe to a man. But before they parted, they foxt *Tarlton* at the Castle in *Pater noster Row,* that *Tarlton* confest them two Tailors to be honest men. So what they spent in the purse, they got in the per|son, Comming but one, by *Tarltons* account, they returned, two. But *Tarlton* comming one, returned lesse by his wit▪ for that was shrunk in the wetting.

36. How *Tarlton* iested at his wife.

TArlton and his wife kéeping an Ordinary in *Paternoster Row,* were bidden out to Supper: and because he was a man noted, shée would not goe with him in the stréet, but intreats him to kéepe one side, and she another: which he consented to. But as he went, hée would cry out to her, and say, Turne that way, wife: and anon, On this side, wife. So the people flockt the more to laugh at them. But his wife (more than mad angry) goes back againe, and almost forswore his company.

37. How *Tarlton* committed a Rakers horse to ward.

WHen *Tarlton* dwelt in *Gracious street,* at a Tauern at the signe of the *Saba,* he was chosen Scauenger, and often the Ward complained of his slacknesse, in kéep|ing the stréets cleane. So on a time when the Cart came, he asked the Raker why he did his businesse so slackly? Sir (said he) my fore-horse was in the fault, who being let bloud and drencht yesterday, I durst not labour him. Sir (said *Tarlton*) your horse shall smart for it: and so leads him to the Counter: which the Raker laught at, and (with|out his horse) did his worke with the rest, thinking *Tarltons*humour was but to iest, and would returne him his horse againe anon. But when that anon came, hée was faine to pay all his fées of the Prison, as directly as if hee himselfe had béene there. For if *Tarlton* had committed the Master, the businesse had not gone forward: therefore the horse was in prison for the Master.

38. How *Tarlton* made *Armin* his adopted sonne to succeed him.

TArlton kéeping a Tauerne in *Gracious-street,* hee let it to another, who was indebted to *Armins* Master, a Goldsmith in *Lombard-street,* yet he himselfe had a cham|ber in the same house. And this *Armin* (being then a wag) came often thither to demand his Masters money, which he sometimes had, and sometimes had not. In the end the man growing poore, told the boy hée had no money for his Master, and hée must beare with him. The mans name being *Charles Armin,* made this Uerse, writing it with Chalke on a Waine-scot.

> O world, why wilt thou lye?
> Is this *Charles* the great? that I deny.
> Indeed *Charles* the great before:
> But now *Charles* the lesse, being poore.

Tarlton comming into the roome, reading it, and partly acquainted with the boyes humour, comming often thither for his Masters money, tooke a péece of Chalk, and wrote this Ryme by it:

> A wagge thou art, none can preuent thee;
> And thy desert shall content thee,
> Let me diuine: As I am, so in time thou'lt be the same,
> My adopted sonne therefore be,
> To enioy my Clownes sute after me.

And sée how it fell out. The boy reading this, so loued *Tarlton* after, that regarding him with more respect, hée vsed to his Playes, and fell in a league with his humour: and priuate practice brought him to present playing, and at this houre performes the same, where, at the *Globe* on the Banks side men may sée him.

39. *Tarltons* greeting with *Banks* his Horse.

THere was one *Banks* (in the time of *Tarlton*) who ser|ued the Earle of *Essex* and had a Horse of strange qua|lities: and being at the Crosse-keyes in *Gracious-street,* getting mony with him, as he was mightily resorted to; *Tarlton* then (with his fellowes) playing at the Bell by, came into the Crosse-keyes (amongst many people (to sée fashions: which *Banks* perceiuing (to make the people laugh) saies *Signior* (to his horse) Go fetch me the veryest foole in the company. The Iade comes immediately, and with his mouth drawes *Tarlton*forth. *Tarlton* (with merry words) said nothing but *God a mercy Horse.* In the end *Tarlton* séeing the people laugh so, was angry inwardly, & said, Sir, had I power of your horse, as you haue, I would doe more than that. What ere it be, said *Banks* (to please him) I will charge him to do it. Then (saies *Tarlton*) charge him to bring me the veriest whore-master in this company. He shall (saies *Bankes,*) *Signior* (saies he) bring Master *Tarlton* here the veriest whore-master in the com|pany. The Horse leades his Master to him. Then god a mercy horse indeed, saies *Tarlton.* The people had much ado to kéep peace; but *Bankes* and *Tarlton* had like to haue squar'd and the horse by to giue aime. But euer after it was a by-word thorow *London, God a mercy Horse,* and is to this day.

40. An excellent Iest of *Tarlton* suddenly spoken.

AT the Bull at Bishops-gate was a Play of *Henry* the fift, wherein the Iudge was to take a box on the eare, and because he was absent that should take the blow, *Tarlton* himselfe (euer forward to please) tooke vpon him to play the same Iudge, besides his owne part of the Clowne: and *Knel* then playing *Henry* the fift, hit *Tarlton* a sound boxe indeed, which made the people laugh the more because it was he: but anon the Iudge goes in, and imme|diately *Tarlton* (in his Clownes cloathes) comes out, and askes the Actors what newes; O (saith one) hadst thou béen here, thou shouldest haue séene Prince *Henry* hit the Iudge a terrible box on the eare. What man, said *Tarlton* strike a Iudge? It is true yfaith, said the other, No other like, said *Tarlton,* and it could not be but terrible to the Iudge, when the report so terrifies me, that me thinkes the blow remaines still on my chéeke, that it burnes againe, The people laught at this mightily: and to this day I haue heard it commended for rare, but no maruell, for he had many of these: But I would sée our Clowns in these dayes doe the like: no I warrant ye, and yet they thinke well of themselues too.

41. *Tarltons* Iest with a Boy in the street.

A Wag-halter Boy met *Tarlton* in the stréet, and said, Master *Tarlton,* who liues longest? Mary Boy, saies *Tarlton,* he that dies latest: and why dye men so fast, said the Boy? Because they want breath, said *Tarlton:* no, ra|ther said the Boy, because their time is come: thē thy time is come, said *Tarlton,* sée who comes yonder: Who? said the Boy? Mary, said *Tarlton, Bull* the Hangman: or one that would willingly be thy hangman: Nay, hang me thē, if I imploy him at this time, said the Boy. Well, said *Tarlton,* then thou wilt be hanged by thy owne confession: and so they parted.

42. A Iest of *Tarlton,* prouing Mustard to haue wit.

TArlton kéeping an Ordinary in Paternoster row and sitting with Gentlemen to make them merry, would approue Mustard (standing before them) to haue wit: how so saies one? It is like a witty scold, méeting another scold, knowing that scold will scold, begins to scold first: so saies he, the Mustard being lickt vp, and knowing that you will bite it, begins to bite you first. Ile try that, saies a Gull by, and the Mustard so tickled him, that his eyes watered. How now, saies *Tarlton,* does my iest sauour? I saies the Gull, and bite too: if you had had better wit, saies *Tarlton,* you would haue bit first: so then conclude with me, hat dumbe vnféeling. Mustard hath more wit than a tal|king vnféeling foole, as you are. Some were pleased, and some were not, but all *Tarltons* care was taken (for his resolution was euer) before he talkt any Iest.

43. How *Tarlton* tooke Tobacco at the first com|ming up of it.

TArlton (as other Gentlemen vsed) at the first comming vp of Tobacco, did take it more for fashions sake then otherwise, and being in a roome, set betwéen two men ouer|come with Wine, and they neuer séeing the like, wondred at it; and séeing the vapour come out of *Tarltons* nose cryed out, Fire, fire, and threw a cup of wine in *Tarltons* face, Make no more stirre, quoth *Tarlton,* the fire is quen|ched: if the Sheriffes come, it will turne to a fine, as the custome is. And drinking that againe, Fie, sayes the other, what a stinke it makes? I am almost poysoned. If it of|fend, saies *Tarlton,* let's euery one take a little of the smell, and so the sauour will quickly goe: but Tobacco whiffes made them leaue him to pay all.

** *Tarltons* pretty Countrey Iests. **

44. *Tarltons* wit betweene a Bird and a Wood-cock.

IN the City of Glocester, M. *Bird* of the Chappell met with *Tarlton,* who ioyfull to regréet other, went to visit his friends: amongst the rest, M. *Bird* of the Quéenes Chappell, visited M. *Wood-cock* of the Colledge, where méeting, many friendly spéeches past, amongst which, M. *Wood-cock* challenged M. *Bird* of Kin: who mused that hee was of his affinity, and hee neuer knew it. Yes sayes M. *Wood-cock,* euery Wood-cock is a Bird, therefore it must needs be so. Lord Sir, sayes *Tarlton,* you are wide, for though euery Wood-cock be a Bird, yet euery Bird is not a Wood-cock. So Master *Wood-cock* like a Wood-cock bit his lip, and mumbudget was silent.

45. *Tarltons* Iest of a Gridiron.

WHile the Quéenes Players lay in Worcester City to get money, it was his custome for to sing *extem|pore* of Theames giuen him: amongst which they were appointed to play the next day: now one fellow of the Ci|ty amongst the rest, that séemed quaint of conceit, to lead other youths with his fine wit, gaue out, that the next day hee would giue him a Theam, to put him to a *non plus:* diuers of his friends acquainted with the same, expected some rare conceit. Well, the next day came, and my Gal|lant gaue him his inuention in two lines, which was this:

> Me thinkes it is a thing vnfit,
> To see a Gridiron turne the Spit.

The people laughed at this, thinking his wit knew no an|swere thereunto, which angred *Tarlton* excéedingly, and presently with a smile looking about, when they expected wonders, he put it off thus.

> Me thinkes it is a thing vnfit:

71

To see an Asse haue any wit.

The people hooted for ioy, to sée the Theame-giuer dasht, who like a dog with his taile betwéene his legs, left the place: But such commendations *Tarlton* got, that hée sapt with the Bailiffe that night, where my Theamer durst not come, although he were sent for, so much he vexed at that vnlookt for answer.

46. *Tarltons* answer in defence of his flat nose.

I Remember I was once at a play in the Country, where as *Tarltons* vse was, the play being done, euery one so pleased to throw vp his Theame: amongst all the rest, one was read to this effect, word by word:

Tarlton, I am one of thy friends, and none of thy foes.

Then I prethee tell how cam'st by thy flat nose:

Had I beene present at that time on those banks,

I would haue laid my short sword ouer his long shankes

Tarlton, mad at this question, as it was his property, sooner to take such a matter ill then well, very suddenly returned him this answere:

> Friend or foe, if thou wilt needs know, marke me well,
> With parting dogs & bears, then by the ears, this chance fell:
> But what of that? though my nose be flat, my credit to saue,
> Yet very well, I can by the smell,
> scent an honest man from a Knave.

47. *Tarltons* Iest of a Bristow man.

WHen the Quéenes Players were restrained in Summer, they trauelled downe to S. *Iames* his Faire, at *Bristow,* where they were worthily entertained both of Londoners, and those Citizens: It hapned that a wealthy Citizen, called M. *Sunbanke,* one morning secretly married his maid; but not so secret, but it was blowne a|broad▪ That morning *Tarlton* and others walking in the Faire to visit his familiar friends of London, & béeing in company of *Bristow* men, they did sée M. *Sunbanke* com|ming, who had his property with his necke, not to stirre it any way but to turne body and all. It chanced at the Faire end, hée stood to pisse against a wall: to whome *Tarlton* came, and clapping him on the shoulder, God giue you joy of your marriage, saies he, M. *Sunbanke,* being taken pis|sing against the wall would haue looked back to thank him, and suddenly turnes about body and all in the view of many, and shewed all: which so abasht him that (ashamed) hée tooke into a Tauerne, protesting that he had rather haue spent ten pound. Sure (said the Uintner) the fault is in your necke, which will not turn without the bodies as|sistance, and not in M. *Tarlton.* Call you him M. *Tarlton,* saies M. *Sunbanke?* Yea, Sir, sayes the Uintner, he is the Quéenes Iester. He may be whose Iester hée will bée, but this iest agrées not with me at this time, saies M. *Sunbanke.*

48. A Iest broke of *Tarlton* by a Country Gentleman.

IN the country where the Quéens Plaiers were accep|ted into a Gentlemans house, the waggon vnlading of the apparell, the wagoner comes to *Tarlton,* and doth de|sire him to speake to the Steward for his horses. I will, saies he: and comming to the Steward, Sir, saies *Tarlton,* where shall our horses spend the time? The Gentleman looking at *Tarlton* at that question suddenly answered, If it please you, or them, let them walke a turne or two, or there is a faire garden, let them play a game or two at bowles in the Alley: and departs thence about his other businesse. *Tarlton* commending the sudden wit of the Steward, saith little. But my Steward not quiet, tels to the Gentlewomen aboue, how he had driuen *Tarlton* to a *non plus* with a iest, whereat they all did laugh heartily: which a Seruingman louing *Tarlton* well, ran and told him as much. *Tarlton,* to adde fuell to the fire, and loth to rest thus put off with a iest, goes and gets two of the horses into the garden, & turnes them into the bowling Alley, who with their héeles made hauock: being the Gentlemans only pastime. The Ladies aboue from a window, seeing horses in the Garden Alley▪ call the Knight, who cries out to *Tarlton,* Fellow, what meanest thou? Nothing Sir, sayes he, but two of my horses are at seuen vp, for a peck of Pro|uender, a foolish match that I made.

Now they being in play at bowles run, run▪ your Steward may come after and cry rub, rub: at which though they smiled, yet the Steward had no thankes for his labour, to set the horses to such an exercise, and they could not blame *Tarlton,* who did but as he was hidden. But by this Iest, oates and hay, stable roome, and all, was plenty.

49. How *Tarlton* made one of his company utterly forsweare drunkennesse.

AT *Salisbury, Tarlton* and his fellowes were to play be|fore the Maior & his brethren: but one of his company (a young man) was so drunke, that he could not: whereat *Tarlton,* as mad angry, as he was mad drunk, claps me on his legs a huge paire of bolts. The fellow dead asléepe, felt nothing. When all was done, they conueyed him to the Iaile on a mans back, and intreated the Iailer to doe God good seruice, and let him lye there till he waked. While they were about their sport the fellow waked, & finding himselfe in durance, and the Iaile hung round with bolts & shackles, he began to blesse himselfe, & thought sure in his drunken|nesse hee had done some mischiefe. With that hee called to know, but none came to him: then hée thought verily his fault was capitall, and that hée was close prisoner. By and by comes the Kéeper, and moaned him, that one so young should come to so shamefull a death as hanging. Anon an|other comes, and another with the like, which further put him in a puzzle. But at last comes *Tarlton,* and others, in|treating the Kéeper, yet if it might bee, that they might sée their fellowere they went. But hée very hardly was in|treated. But at length the poore drunken Signior cald out for them. In they come. Oh *Tom,* sayes *Tarlton,* hard was thy hap, in drunkennesse to murder this honest man, & our hard hap too, to haue it reported, any of our company is hang'd for it. O God, O God, saies the fellow, is my fault so great? then commend mée to all my friends. Well short tale to make, the fellow forswore drunkennesse, if hée could escape, and by as cunning a wile (to his thinking) they got him out of prison by an escape, and sent him to London be|fore, who was not a little glad to be gone. But sée how this iest wrought: by little & little the fellow left his excessiue drinking, and in time altered his desire of drunkennesse.

50. How *Tarlton* saued his head from cutting off.

TArlton vpon a time being in the Country, and lodging in an homely Inne, during which time there was a Gentleman dwelling in the same towne, somewhat fran|ticke and distraught of his wits: which mad-man on a sudden rusht into *Tarltons* bed-chamber, with his sword drawne, and finding him there in bed, would haue slaine him: saying, Uillaine, were it not valiantly done to strike off thy knaues head at one blow? *Tarlton* answered. Tut, Sir, that's nothing with your Worship to doe: you can as easily strike off two heads at one blow, as one: wherefore, if you please, Ile goe downe and call vp another, and so you may strike off both our heads at once. The mad man beléeued him, and so let him slip away.

51. How *Tarlton* escaped imprisonment.

TArlton hauing béen dominéering very late one night, with two of his friends, and comming homewards a|long Cheape-side, the watch being then set, M. Constable asked, Who goes there? Thrée merry men, quoth *Tarlton*. That is not sufficient. What are you, qd. M. Constable? Why, saies *Tarlton,* one of vs is an eye-maker, and the other a light-maker. What saiest thou, knaue, doest mocke mée? the one is an eye-maker, the other a light-maker, which two properties belong vnto God only: commit these blasphemers, quoth the constable. Nay, I pray you good M. Constable, be good in your Office, I will approue what I haue said, to be true qd. *Tarlton*. If thou canst saies the Con|stable, you shall passe, otherwise you shall be all thrée puni|shed. Why (qd. *Tarlton*) this fellow is an ey-maker, be|cause a Spectacle-maker; and this other a maker of light, because a Chādler, that makes your darkest night as light as your Lanthorn. The Constable séeing them so pleasant, was well contented. The rest of the watchmen laughed: & *Tarlton* with his two companions went home quietly.

52. How *Tarlton* deceived a Country Wench.

THe Quéens players trauelling into the west Country to play, and lodging in a little Uillage, some ten miles from *Bristow,* in which village dwelt a pretty nut-browne Lasse, to whome *Tarlton* made proffer of marriage, prote|sted, that he came from London purposely to marry her. The simple maid being proud to bée beloued by such a one whom she knew to bée the Quéenes man, without more intreatie, yéelded: and being both at the Church together, and M. Parson ready to performe his duty, and comming to the words of, I *Richard* take thée *Ioane:* nay, stay good Master Parson, I will go and call my fellowes, and come to you again: so going out of the Church in haste, he retur|ned at leasure; for, hauing his horse ready saddled, he rode toward Bristow, and by the way told his fellowes of his successe with his Wench.

53. How *Tarlton* went to kill Crowes.

IT chanced vpon a time, as *Tarlton* went foorth with a Birding péece into the fields to kill Crowes, hee spied a Daw sitting in a trée, at which he meant to shoot; but at the same instant, there came one by, to whome hée spake in this manner: Sir quoth he, yonder I sée a Daw, which I will shoot at if she sit. If she sit, said the other, then she is a Daw indéed: but, quoth *Tarlton,* if shee sit not, what is she then? Marry, quoth the other, a Daw also: at which words she immediately flew away: whereupon, *Tarlton* spake merrily in a Rime, as followeth:

> Whether a Daw sit, or whether a Daw fly,
> Whether a Daw stand, or whether a Daw lye,
> Whether a Daw creepe, or whether a Daw cry,
> In what case soever a Daw persever,
> A Daw is a Daw, and a Daw shall be ever.

54. How a poore Begger-man ouer-reached *Tarlton* by his wit.

AS *Tarlton* vpon a day sate at his owne doore, to him came a poore old man & begged a peny for the Lords sake: whereupon *Tarlton* hauing no single money about him, askt the begger what mony he had? No more mony, Master, but one single peny. *Tarlton,* being merrily dispo|sed called for his peny, and hauing receiued it, gaue it to his Boy to fetch a pot of Ale: whereat the begger grew blanke, and began to gather vp his wits, how to get it a|gain: the pot of Ale, for the beggers peny, being brought, he proffered to drinke to the Begger. Nay, stay awhile Master, quoth the Begger, the vse is, where I was borne, that hee that payes for the drink, must drink first. Thou saist well, quoth *Tarlton*; goe to, Drink to me then. Where|vpon the begger tooke the Pot, saying, Here, Master, I drink to you, (& therewithall dranke off euery drop.) Now Master, if you will pledge me, send for it as I haue done. *Tarlton* séeing himselfe so ouer-reacht, greatly commended the Beggers wit, and withall in recompence thereof, gaue him a Teaster: with that the Begger said, that hée would most truly pray to God for him. No, answered *Tarlton,* I pray thée pray for thy selfe, for I take no vsury for almes-déeds.

55. Of *Tarltons* pleasant answer to a Gallant by the high-way side.

IT was *Tarltons* occasion another time to ride into Suf|folk, being furnished with a very leane large horse: and by the way, a lusty Gallant met him; and in mockage asked him, what a yard of his horse was worth? Marry Sir, quoth *Tarlton,* I pray you alight, and lift vp my horses Taile, and they in that shop will tell you the price of a yard.

56. How *Tarlton* would haue drowned his Wife.

VPon a time, as *Tarlton* and his Wife, (as passengers) came sailing from Southampton towards London, a mighty storme arose, and endangered the Ship, where|vpon, the Captaine thereof charged euery man to throw into the Seas the heauiest thing hée could best spare, to the end to lighten some-what the Ship. *Tarlton,* that had his Wife there, offered to throw her ouer-boord: but the com|pany rescued her; and being asked wherefore he meant so to doe? he answered, She is the heauiest thing I haue, and I can best spare her.

57. How *Tarlton* made his Will and Testament.

OF late there was a Gentlman liuing in England, that wheresoeuer he dined, would of euery dish con|ney a modicum thereof into his Gowne sléeue: which Gentleman being vpon a time at dinner at a Gentlemans house in the Country, there he vsed his aforesaid quality, in the company of Master *Tarlton,* who perceiuing it, said thus vnto the company: My Masters, I am now determi|ned before you all, to make my last Will and Testament: And first, I bequeath my soule to God my Creator, and my body to be buried in the sléeue of yonder Gentlemans Gowne, and with that, stepping to him, he turned vp the Gowne sléeue, whereout, here dropt a bit, and there a bit, with choice of much other good chéere, still shaking it, saying, I meant this sléeue, Gentlman, this sléeue I meant.

58. How *Tarlton* called a Gentleman knave by craft.

WIthin a while after, as the same Gentleman and *Tarlton* passed thorow a field together, a Crow in a Trée cried Kaw, Kaw, See yonder *Tarlton,* quoth the Gentleman yonder Crow calleth thée knaue. No, Sir (he answered) he beckens to your Worship as the better man.

59. *Tarltons* Iest of a Country Wench.

TArlton going towards Hogsdon, met a country maid comming to market, her Mare stumbling, downe shée fell ouer and ouer, shewing all that euer God sent her, and then rising vp againe, shée turned her round about vnto Master *Tarlton,* and said, Gods body Sir, Did you euer sée the like before? No, in good sooth, quoth *Tarlton,* neuer but once in London.

60. How *Tarlton* deceived an Inne-holder at Sandwich.

VPon a time, when the Plaiers were put to silence, *Tarlton* & his Boy frollickt so long in the Countrey, that all their money was gone, and béeing a great way from London, they knew not what to doe; but as want is the whetstone of wit, *Tarlton* gathered his conceits toge|ther, and practised a trick to beare him vp to London without money, and thus it was: Unto an Inne in Sand|wich they went, and there lay for two daies at great charge, although he had no money to pay for the same:

the third morning he bade his man goe downe, and male-con|tent
himself before his host and his hostesse, and mum|bling say to himself,
Lord, Lord, what a scald Master doe I serue? this it is to serue such
Seminary Priests and Ie|suites: now euen as I am an honest Boy, Ile
leaue him in the lurch, and shift for my selfe: heres adoe about Pe|nance
and Mortification, as though (forsooth) Christ hath not dyed enough
for all. The Boy mumbled out these his instructions so dissembling,
that it strooke a iealously in the Inne-holders heart, that out of doubt
his master was a Seminarie Priest; whereupon, he presently sent for the
Constable, and told him all the foresaid matter & so went vp both
together to attache *Tarlton* in his chamber, who purposely had shut
himself close in, and betaken him to his knées, & to his crosses, to make
the matter séeme more su|spitious: which they espying through the
key-hole, made no more adoe, but in they rushed, & arrested him for
a Se|minarie Priest, discharged his score, bore his, & his boyes charges
vp to London, and there in hope to haue rich re|wards, presented
him to *M. Fleetwood,* the old Recorder of London: but now marke
the Iest; when the Recorder saw *Tarlton,* and knew him passing well,
entertained him very courteously, and all to befool'd the Inne-holder,
& his mate, and sent them away whith fleas in their eares: but when
Tarlton sawe himselfe discharged out of their hand he stood iesting and
pointing at their folly, and so taught them by cunning, more wit and
thrift against ano|ther time.

61. Of *Tarltons* Wrongfull accusation.

VPon a time *Tarlton* was wrongfully accused for get|ting of a
Gentlemans Maid with child and for the same, brought before a Iustice
in *Kent,* which Iustice said as followeth: It is a mervalle *(M. Tarlton)*
that you being a Gentleman of good qualitie, and one of her Maiesties
servants, would venture thus to get Maides with childe. Nay rather
(quoth *Tarlton*) were it maruell, if a maid had gotten me with child.

62. *Tarlton* deceived by a Country wench.

TArlton trauelling to play abroad, was in a Towne where in the Inne was a pretty maid, whose fauour was placed in a corner of *Tarltons*affection: and talking with her, shée appoynted to méet him at the bottom of a paire of staires. Night and the houre came, and the maid subtilly sent downe her Mistresse: whome *Tarlton* catching in his armes, Art come, wench, saies hée? Out alas, sayes the Mistres, not knowing who it was. *Tarlton* hearing it was the Mistres, start aside, and the maid came downe with a candle, and shée espyde a glimpse of *Tarlton* in the darke, who stept into another roome. How now, Mistres, said the maid? Something (said shée) affrighted me, some man sure, for I heard him speake. No, no, Mistresse, said the Maid, it is no man, it was a Bull calf that I shut in|to a roome, till *Iohn* our Pounder came to haue pounded him for a stray. Had I thought that (saith she) I would haue bit him such a knocke on his forehead, that his hornes should never have grac'd his Coxcombe, and so she departs vp againe afra●id. But how *Tarlton* tooke this iest, think you.

63. How *Tarlton* could not abide a Cat, and deceiued himselfe.

IN the Country *Tarlton* told his Oastesse he was a Con|iurer. O sir (sayes she) I had pewter stolne off my shelfe the other day, help me to it, and I will forgiue you all the pots of Ale you owe mee, which is sixteene dozen. Sayes *Tarlton,* To morrow morning the Diuell shall helpe you to it, or I will trounce him. Morning came, and the Oa|stesse and he met in a roome by themselues. *Tarlton,* to passe the time with exercise of his wit, with Circles and tricks falls to coniure, hauing no more skill then a dogge. But sée the iest, how contrarily it fell out: as he was cal|ling out, *mons, pons, simul & fons,* and such like, a Cat (vnexpected) leapt from the gutter window, which sight so amazed *Tarlton,* that he skipt thence, & threw his Hostesse downe, so that he departed with his fellowes, and left her hip out of ioynt, being then in the Surgeons hands, and not daring to tell how it came.

64. How *Tarlton* and his Oastesse of *Waltham* met.

TArlton riding with divers Citizens his friends, to make merry at *Waltham,* by the way he met with his Oastesse riding toward *London,* whome hée of old acquain|tance saluted. Shée demands whither they went? *Tarlton* told her, to make merry at *Waltham.* Sir (saies she) then let me request your company at my house at the *Christo|pher,* and (for old familiarity) spend your money there. Not vnlesse you goe backe (saies *Tarlton*) we will else goe to the *Hound.* But she (loth to lose their custome) sent to *London* by her man, & goes back with them, who by the way had much mirth, for she was an excéeding merry honest womā, yet would take any thing: which *Tarlton* hearing, as wise as he was (thinking her of his minde) he was deceiued: yet he askt her if the biggest bed in her house were able to hold two of their bignesse (meaning himself & her?) Yes (saies she) and tumble vp and downe at pleasure. Yea, one vpon another, saies *Tarlton?* And vnder too, saies she. Well, to haue their custome, she agreed to euery thing, like a subtill Oastesse: and it fell so out that *Tarlton* hauing her in a roome at her house, askt her which of those two beds were big enough for them two? This, said she: therefore goe to bed sweet-heart, Ile come to thee. Masse (saies *Tarlton*) were my Bootes off, I would indeed. I'le help you, Sir (saies she) if you please. Yea (thought *Tarlton*) is the wind in that doore? come on then. And she very diligently begins to pull, till one boot was half off. Now (saies she) this be|ing hard to doe, let me try my cunning on the other, and so get off both. But hauing both half off his legs, she left him alone in the Shoomakers stocks, and got her to *London,* where *Tarlton,* was three houres, and had no help. But being eas'd of his paine, he made this Ryme for a Theame, singing of it all the way to London:

Women are Wanton, and hold it no sinne,
By tricks and devices to pull a man in.

65. *Tarltons* meeting with his Countrey acquaintance at *Ilford.*

ON a Sunday, *Tarlton* rode to *Ilford,* where his father kept: and dining with him at his Sisters, there came in diuers of the Countrey to see him, amongst whom was one plaine Countrey plough-iogger, who said hee was of *Tarltons* kin, & so called him cousin. But *Tarlton* demanded of his father if it were so? but he knew no such matter; whereupon saies *Tarlton,* whether he be of my kin or no, I will be cousin to him ere we part, if all the drinke in *Ilford* will doe it. So vpon this they caroused fréely, & the Clowne was then in his Cue so that (in briefe) they were both in soundly. Night came & *Tarlton* would not let his cousin goe, but they would lye together that night, meaning to drinke at their departure next morning. *Tarlton* would by wit leaue him in the lash, since power would not. But sée the jest: That night the plaine fellow so pist *Tarlton* in his bed, thinking he had béen against the Church wal, that he was faine to cry for a fresh shirt to shift him. So when al was well, they must néeds drinke at parting: where indéed (to seale kindred soundly) the fellow h•d his loade: for hea|ring that his cousin *Tarlton,* was gone to *London,* zounds he would follow, that he would, none could hold him: and meaning to goe towards *London,* his aime was so good, that he went towards *Rumford* to sell his Hogs.

66. How a Maid drave *Tarlton* to a Non-plus.

TArlton méeting with a wily Country wench, who gaue him quip for quip; Swéet heart (said hée) would my flesh were in thine. So would I, Sir (saies shee) I would your nose were in my, I know where. *Tarlton* an|gred at this, said no more; but goes forward.

67. *Tarltons* answere to a question.

ONe asked *Tarltō* why Munday was called Sundaies fellow? Because he is a sausie fellow (saies *Tarlton*) to compare with that holy day. But if may be, Munday thinkes himselfe Sundayes fellow, because it followes Sunday, and is next after: but he comes a day after the Faire for that. Nay (saies the fellow) but if two Sun|dayes fall together, Munday then may be the first, and it would shew well too. Yes (saies *Tarlton*) but if thy nose stood vnder thy mouth, it would shew better, and be more for thy profit. How for my profit, said the fellow? Marry (said *Tarlton*) neuer to be cold in winter, being so néere euery dogs taile. The fellow séeing a foolish question had a foolish answere, laid his legges on his neck, and got him gone.

68. *Tarltons* desire of enough for money.

TArlton comming into a Market towne bought Oates for his horse, and desired enough for money: the man said. You shall, Sir and gaue him two halfe pecks for one. *Tarlton* thought his Horse should that night fare largely, and comes to him with this Rime:

Iack Nag, he brag, and lustie braue it,
I have enough for mony, and thou shalt have it.

But when *Iack Nag* smelt to them, they were so musty, that he would none (God thanke you, Master) which *Tarlton* séeing, runnes into the Market, and would slash and cut. But til the next Market day the fellow was not to be found, and before then *Tarlton* must be gone.

69. How *Tarltons* Dogge lickt vp six pence.

TArlton in his Trauaile had a Dogge of fine qualities, amongst the rest, he would carry six pence in the end of his tongue, of which he would brag often, and say, Never was the like. Yes, saies a Lady, mine is more strange, for he will beare a French crowne in his mouth: no, saies *Tarlton,* I thinke not: lend me a French crowne, saies the Lady, and you shall sée: truly Madame, I haue it not but if your dog will carry a crackt English crowne, here if is but the Lady perceiued not the iest, but was desirous to see the dogs trick of six pence. *Tarlton* threw down a teaster, and said, Bring Sirra: and by fortune the Dog took vp a Counter, and let the money lie: a Gentlewoman by, séeing that, askt him how long he would hold it? An houre, saies *Tarlto:* that is pretty, said the Gentlewoman, let's sée that: meane time she tooke vp the sixe pence, and willed him to let them sée the money againe: when he did sée it, it was a Counter, and he made this Rime.

Alas, alas, how came all this to passe?
The worlds worse then it was:
For silver turns to brasse.

I, sayes the Lady, & the dog hath made his master an Asse: but *Tarlton* would never trust to his Dogs tricks more.

70. *Tarltons* Iest of a Horse and a Man.

IN the City of Norwich, *Tarlton* was on a time inuited to an hunting: where there was a goodly Gentlewoman, that brauely mounted on a blacke horse, rode excéeding well, to the wonder of all the beholders, and neither hedge nor ditch stood in her way, but *Pegasus* her horse (for so may we tearme him for swiftnesse) flew ouer all, and she sate him aswell. When euery one returned home, some at Supper commended his Hound, others his Hawke, and shée aboue all, her Horse: and, said she, I loue no liuing creature so well (at this instant) as my gallant horse: yes Lady, a man better, saies *Tarlton*. Indéed no, said shée, not now: For since my last husband dyed, I hate them most, vnlesse you can giue me medicines to make me loue them. *Tarlton* made this iest instantly:

Why, a Horse mingeth Whay, Madam, a Man min|geth Amber,
A Horse is for your Way, Madam, but a man for your Chamber.

God a mercy, *Tarlton,* said the men: which the Gentle|woman noting, séeing they tooke exceptions at her words, to make all well, answered thus:

That a Horse is my chiefe opinion now, I deny not,
And when a man doth me more good in my chamber, I him defie not.

But till then give me leaue to loue something: then some|thing will please you, said *Tarlton,* I am glad of that, there|fore I pray God send you a good thing, or none at all.

71. *Tarltons* talke with a pretty Woman.

GEntlewoman, said *Tarlton,* and the rest as you sit, I can tell you strange things: now many Gallants at Supper noted one woman, who being little and pretty, to vnfit her prettinesse, had a great wide mouth, which she sée|ming to hide, would pinch in her spéeches, and speake small, but was desirous to heare newes. *Tarlton* told at his comming from London to Norwich, a Proclamation was made that euery man should haue two wiues. now *Iesus,* qd. she is it possible? I Gentlewoman, and other wise able too, for contrarily women haue a larger préeminence, for euery woman must haue thrée husbands: Now *Iawsus,* said the Gentlewoman, and with wonder shewes the full wide|nesse of her mouth, which all the table smil'd at: which she perceiuing, would answere no more. Now Mistris, said, *Tarlton,* your mouth is lesse then euer it was, for now it is able to say nothing. Thou art a cogging Knaue, said she. Masse, and that is somthing yet, said *Tarlton,* your mouth shall be as wide as euer it was, for that Iest.

72. A Iest of *Tarlton* to a great man.

THere was a great huge man, 3. yards in the wast, at *S. Edmondsbury* in *Suffolk,* that died but of late daies (one *M. Blague* by name) & a good kinde Iustice too, carefull for the poore, this Iustice met with *Tarlton* in Norwich: *Tarlton,* said he, Giue me thy hand: But, you Sir, being richer, may giue me a greater gift, giue me your body: and imbracing him, could not halfe compasse him: being merry in talke, said the Iustice: *Tarlton,* tell me one thing, what is the difference betwixt a Flea and a Louse? Marry, Sir; said *Tarlton,* as much and like difference, as twixt you and me: I like a Flea sée else) can skip nimbly: But you, like a fat Louse créepe slowly, and you can go no faster, though Butchers are ouer you, ready to knock you on the head. Thou art a knaue, quoth the Iustice. I, Sir, I knew that ere I came hither, else I had not béen here now, for euer one knaue (making a stop) séekes out another. The Iustice vnderstanding him▪ laughed heartily.

73. *Tarltons* Iest to a maid in the darke.

TArlton going in the darke, groping out his way, heares the tread of some one to méet him. Who goes there, saies he? A man, or a monster? said the maid, A monster: said *Tarlton,* A candle hoe: and séeing who it was, Indéed said he, A monster, Ile be sworne: for thy téeth are longer then thy heard, O Sir, said the maid, speake no more then you see, for women goe inuisible now adayes.

74. *Tarltons* Iest to a Dogge.

TArlton and his fellows, being in the Bishop of Wor|cesters Seller, and being largely laid to, *Tarlton* had his rouse, and going through the streets, a Dogge (in the middle of the street, asleep, on a dunghill) seeing *Tarlton* reele on him, on the suddaine barkt, How now Dog, saies *Tarlton,* are you in your humors? and many daies after it was a by-word to a man being drunke, that he was in his humors.

FINIS.

Source:

**https://quod.lib.umich.edu/e/eebo/
A13376.0001.001?rgn=main;view=fulltext**

APPENDIX B: BIBLIOGRAPHY

Cunningham, Peter, 1816-1869, editor. *Revels at Court: Being Extracts from the Revels Accounts of the Reigns of Queen Elizabeth and James.* London: Printed for the Shakespeare Society, 1853.
https://tinyurl.com/ybnfcxzo

Hazlitt, W. Carew, editor. *Shakespeare Jest-Books; Reprints of the Early and Very Rare Jest-Books Supposed to have been Used by Shakespeare.* Volume 2 (of 3). London, Willis & Sotheran, 1864.
https://tinyurl.com/ycjv9y7o

***

Full text of *Tarlton's Jests, and News out of purgatory*:[1]
https://archive.org/stream/tarltonsjestsan00chetgoog/tarltonsjestsan00chetgoog_djvu.txt

***

Full text of *Tarlton's Jests*
https://quod.lib.umich.edu/e/eebo/A13376.0001.001?rgn=main;view=fulltext

***

Here are biographical notes on Tarlton:
http://qme.internetshakespeare.uvic.ca/Foyer/biopages/RichardTarlton.html

---

1. https://archive.org/details/tarltonsjestsan00chetgoog

APPENDIX C: ABOUT THE AUTHOR

It was a dark and stormy night. Suddenly a cry rang out, and on a hot summer night in 1954, Josephine, wife of Carl Bruce, gave birth to a boy — me. Unfortunately, this young married couple allowed Reuben Saturday, Josephine's brother, to name their first-born. Reuben, aka "The Joker," decided that Bruce was a nice name, so he decided to name me Bruce Bruce. I have gone by my middle name — David — ever since.

Being named Bruce David Bruce hasn't been all bad. Bank tellers remember me very quickly, so I don't often have to show an ID. It can be fun in charades, also. When I was a counselor as a teenager at Camp Echoing Hills in Warsaw, Ohio, a fellow counselor gave the signs for "sounds like" and "two words," then she pointed to a bruise on her leg twice. Bruise Bruise? Oh yeah, Bruce Bruce is the answer!

Uncle Reuben, by the way, gave me a haircut when I was in kindergarten. He cut my hair short and shaved a small bald spot on the back of my head. My mother wouldn't let me go to school until the bald spot grew out again.

Of all my brothers and sisters (six in all), I am the only transplant to Athens, Ohio. I was born in Newark, Ohio, and have lived all around Southeastern Ohio. However, I moved to Athens to go to Ohio University and have never left.

At Ohio U, I never could make up my mind whether to major in English or Philosophy, so I got a Bachelor's with a double major in both areas in 1980, then I added a Master's in English in 1984 and a Master's in Philosophy in 1985. Currently, I am a retired English instructor at Ohio U.

If all goes well, I will publish one or two books a year for the rest of my life. (On the other hand, a good way to make God laugh is to tell Her your plans.)

By the way, my sister Brenda Kennedy writes romances such as *A New Beginning* and *Shattered Dreams*.

APPENDIX D: SOME BOOKS BY DAVID BRUCE

Retellings of a Classic Work of Literature
Arden of Faversham: *A Retelling*
Ben Jonson's The Alchemist: *A Retelling*
Ben Jonson's The Arraignment, or Poetaster: *A Retelling*
Ben Jonson's Bartholomew Fair: *A Retelling*
Ben Jonson's The Case is Altered: *A Retelling*
Ben Jonson's Catiline's Conspiracy: *A Retelling*
Ben Jonson's The Devil is an Ass: *A Retelling*
Ben Jonson's Epicene: *A Retelling*
Ben Jonson's Every Man in His Humor: *A Retelling*
Ben Jonson's Every Man Out of His Humor: *A Retelling*
Ben Jonson's The Fountain of Self-Love, or Cynthia's Revels: *A Retelling*
Ben Jonson's The Magnetic Lady, or Humors Reconciled: *A Retelling*
Ben Jonson's The New Inn, or The Light Heart: *A Retelling*
Ben Jonson's Sejanus' Fall: *A Retelling*
Ben Jonson's The Staple of News: *A Retelling*
Ben Jonson's A Tale of a Tub: *A Retelling*
Ben Jonson's Volpone, or the Fox: *A Retelling*
Christopher Marlowe's Complete Plays: Retellings
Christopher Marlowe's Dido, Queen of Carthage: *A Retelling*
Christopher Marlowe's Doctor Faustus: *Retellings of the 1604 A-Text and of the 1616 B-Text*
Christopher Marlowe's Edward II: *A Retelling*
Christopher Marlowe's The Massacre at Paris: *A Retelling*
Christopher Marlowe's The Rich Jew of Malta: *A Retelling*
Christopher Marlowe's Tamburlaine, Parts 1 and 2: *Retellings*
Dante's Divine Comedy: *A Retelling in Prose*
Dante's Inferno: *A Retelling in Prose*
Dante's Purgatory: *A Retelling in Prose*
Dante's Paradise: *A Retelling in Prose*
The Famous Victories of Henry V: *A Retelling*
From the Iliad *to the* Odyssey: *A Retelling in Prose of Quintus of Smyrna's* Posthomerica
George Chapman, Ben Jonson, and John Marston's Eastward Ho! *A Retelling*

George Peele's The Arraignment of Paris: *A Retelling*

George Peele's The Battle of Alcazar: *A Retelling*

George Peele's David and Bathsheba, and the Tragedy of Absalom: *A Retelling*

George Peele's Edward I: *A Retelling*

George Peele's The Old Wives' Tale: *A Retelling*

George-a-Greene: *A Retelling*

The History of King Leir: *A Retelling*

Homer's Iliad: *A Retelling in Prose*

Homer's Odyssey: *A Retelling in Prose*

J.W. Gent.'s The Valiant Scot: *A Retelling*

Jason and the Argonauts: A Retelling in Prose of Apollonius of Rhodes' Argonautica

John Ford: Eight Plays Translated into Modern English

John Ford's The Broken Heart: *A Retelling*

John Ford's The Fancies, Chaste and Noble: *A Retelling*

John Ford's The Lady's Trial: *A Retelling*

John Ford's The Lover's Melancholy: *A Retelling*

John Ford's Love's Sacrifice: *A Retelling*

John Ford's Perkin Warbeck: *A Retelling*

John Ford's The Queen: *A Retelling*

John Ford's 'Tis Pity She's a Whore: *A Retelling*

John Lyly's Campaspe: *A Retelling*

John Lyly's Endymion, The Man in the Moon: *A Retelling*

John Lyly's Galatea: *A Retelling*

John Lyly's Love's Metamorphosis: *A Retelling*

John Lyly's Midas: *A Retelling*

John Lyly's Mother Bombie: *A Retelling*

John Lyly's Sappho and Phao: *A Retelling*

John Lyly's The Woman in the Moon: *A Retelling*

John Webster's The White Devil: *A Retelling*

King Edward III: *A Retelling*

Mankind: *A Medieval Morality Play* (A Retelling)

Margaret Cavendish's The Unnatural Tragedy: *A Retelling*

The Merry Devil of Edmonton: *A Retelling*

The Summoning of Everyman: *A Medieval Morality Play* (A Retelling)

Robert Greene's Friar Bacon and Friar Bungay: *A Retelling*

The Taming of a Shrew: *A Retelling*

Tarlton's Jests: A Retelling

Thomas Middleton's A Chaste Maid in Cheapside: *A Retelling*

Thomas Middleton's Women Beware Women: *A Retelling*

Thomas Middleton and Thomas Dekker's The Roaring Girl: *A Retelling*
Thomas Middleton and William Rowley's The Changeling: *A Retelling*
The Trojan War and Its Aftermath: Four Ancient Epic Poems
Virgil's Aeneid: *A Retelling in Prose*
William Shakespeare's 5 Late Romances: Retellings in Prose
William Shakespeare's 10 Histories: Retellings in Prose
William Shakespeare's 11 Tragedies: Retellings in Prose
William Shakespeare's 12 Comedies: Retellings in Prose
William Shakespeare's 38 Plays: Retellings in Prose
William Shakespeare's 1 Henry IV, aka Henry IV, Part 1: A Retelling in Prose
William Shakespeare's 2 Henry IV, aka Henry IV, Part 2: A Retelling in Prose
William Shakespeare's 1 Henry VI, aka Henry VI, Part 1: A Retelling in Prose
William Shakespeare's 2 Henry VI, aka Henry VI, Part 2: A Retelling in Prose
William Shakespeare's 3 Henry VI, aka Henry VI, Part 3: A Retelling in Prose
William Shakespeare's All's Well that Ends Well: *A Retelling in Prose*
William Shakespeare's Antony and Cleopatra: *A Retelling in Prose*
William Shakespeare's As You Like It: *A Retelling in Prose*
William Shakespeare's The Comedy of Errors: *A Retelling in Prose*
William Shakespeare's Coriolanus: *A Retelling in Prose*
William Shakespeare's Cymbeline: *A Retelling in Prose*
William Shakespeare's Hamlet: *A Retelling in Prose*
William Shakespeare's Henry V: *A Retelling in Prose*
William Shakespeare's Henry VIII: *A Retelling in Prose*
William Shakespeare's Julius Caesar: *A Retelling in Prose*
William Shakespeare's King John: *A Retelling in Prose*
William Shakespeare's King Lear: *A Retelling in Prose*
William Shakespeare's Love's Labor's Lost: *A Retelling in Prose*
William Shakespeare's Macbeth: *A Retelling in Prose*
William Shakespeare's Measure for Measure: *A Retelling in Prose*
William Shakespeare's The Merchant of Venice: *A Retelling in Prose*
William Shakespeare's The Merry Wives of Windsor: *A Retelling in Prose*
William Shakespeare's A Midsummer Night's Dream: *A Retelling in Prose*
William Shakespeare's Much Ado About Nothing: *A Retelling in Prose*
William Shakespeare's Othello: *A Retelling in Prose*
William Shakespeare's Pericles, Prince of Tyre: *A Retelling in Prose*
William Shakespeare's Richard II: *A Retelling in Prose*
William Shakespeare's Richard III: *A Retelling in Prose*
William Shakespeare's Romeo and Juliet: *A Retelling in Prose*
William Shakespeare's The Taming of the Shrew: *A Retelling in Prose*

William Shakespeare's The Tempest: *A Retelling in Prose*
William Shakespeare's Timon of Athens: *A Retelling in Prose*
William Shakespeare's Titus Andronicus: *A Retelling in Prose*
William Shakespeare's Troilus and Cressida: *A Retelling in Prose*
William Shakespeare's Twelfth Night: *A Retelling in Prose*
William Shakespeare's The Two Gentlemen of Verona: *A Retelling in Prose*
William Shakespeare's The Two Noble Kinsmen: *A Retelling in Prose*
William Shakespeare's The Winter's Tale: *A Retelling in Prose*

www.ingramcontent.com/pod-product-compliance
Lightning Source LLC
Chambersburg PA
CBHW022205150726
47992CB00002B/968